Alternate Timeline

Alternate Timeline

Stanton Call

Yazdan Publishing

Alternate Timeline

Yazdan Publishing First Printing, November 2023

Printed in the United States of America

ISBN-13: 978-1-938838-19-4

Yazdan Publishing
P O Box 56545
Virginia Beach, VA 23456

"The distinction between the past, the present, and the future is only a stubbornly persistent illusion."
Albert Einstein

To be sure, the existence of an alternate timeline has caused some measure of apprehension for every member of the League. Not only does such a timeline possess the potential of taking supremacy over our own but the Governor-General — truly the entire Core — now believes that our greatest threat may be the personal "duplicates" that inevitably exist in such a place. What is to prevent them from leaving their own timeline and coming to ours here on the ATL? Should we dare to consider that such has already occurred?

Certainly, the fact that Emma #119 was taken from us has only heightened the likelihood that rebel Time Travelers now traverse between alternate timelines with relative ease. Such a possibility has prompted me to consider whether there might already be Wayfarers among us who are not who they profess to be.

Ben #239, Wayfarer

It is extremely difficult for even the most experienced Time Traveler to fully comprehend the fact that time cannot exist without a consciousness to perceive it. Truly, observing the dynamics of time and its apparent past, present, and unfolding future is fundamental to the human experience, but ultimately, time is nothing more than a perceptual illusion.

When Moment One gave birth to space-time, it initiated the experience of limited consciousness perceiving the third-dimensional plane. It created the ability for individuals to observe the consequences of personal actions upon a linear timeline. It produced the interaction between cause and effect and provided a means to gauge the growth of individual awareness. However, each of these perceived outcomes is ultimately no more real than the illusion of space-time that created them.

Excerpt, "Preface," *Wayfarer's Manual — Continuing Education (revised edition);* **by Ruth #7**

ONE: Journal Entry — December 9 ATL

I am a Time Traveler. In actual fact, I am officially a Wayfarer graduate. This journal constitutes the third volume detailing my experiences with the League and our time-traveling profession. In spite of a well-deserved graduation, however, my four classmates and I have already been apprised of the fact that we will continue to meet with our instructress, Agnes #23, two nights per week regarding the matter of our ongoing Wayfarer education. The frustration over this unexpected development was perhaps best expressed for us all when my assigned roomie George, stated only, "You have got to be kidding!" Shortly thereafter, Agnes was quick to provide us with— what she seems most fond of describing as—our "REQUIRED continuing education manual." Setting aside the lingering annoyance of such surprising news, I should note herein all that has transpired since our commencement ceremony and the graduation banquet which followed that selfsame day.

The Governor-General, Sara #11, chose to distribute our graduation diplomas in alphabetical order, taking occasion to give the five of us recognition for the core purpose of our time-traveling endeavors since the start of our education. She began with me, "Ben #239," and proceeded to acknowledge my "remarkable proficiency with diplomacy." Next came our French classmate, Bonne Soeur Marie, who was recognized for "her skills in healing and medicine." Emanuel, our attentive Swede scholar, was thanked for his commitment to matters dealing with "both spiritual enlightenment and personal transformation." My dear friend and occasional roommate, George, was congratulated for his ongoing efforts as a "most dedicated philanthropist." And finally, the Governor-General called upon our Latin peer, Manuela, and gave public appreciation for her work "with the underprivileged and those who seek equality."

After these brief acknowledgments had been communicated to all present, Agnes rose to the podium, unfolded a piece of paper retrieved from her dress pocket, bobbed about before us with more theatrical flair than seemed appropriate for such an occasion, and began reading aloud each of our forthcoming time traveling assignments.

"Ben #239, destination Washington, DC, 1941, in the

matter of Eleanor Roosevelt, and her destiny as global ambassador."

"Bonne Soeur Marie #304, destination London, King's College, 2054, in the matter of the eradication of cancer."

"Emanuel #41, destination Vatican City, 2123, in the matter of the reunification of Eastern Orthodoxy and Catholicism."

"George #111, destination the Philippines, 2020, in the matter of philanthropic endeavors to address a coronavirus."

"Manuela #64, destination Babylon, 539 BC, in the matter of Cyrus the Great, and the emancipation of slaves."

Immediately after these projects had been announced, and we had reconvened in the League Café for the celebratory banquet that followed, a surprise visitor in the form of Gregory #143 appeared before us. For many of those present, the surprise was threefold. In the first, it was assumed that Gregory had already been eradicated from the approved timeline (ATL) by Ruth #7 herself for his crime of abandoning the League. To be sure, my roomie and I knew this not to be the case as Ruth had sworn the two of us to secrecy in the matter of her plan to find Emmett—the Core's former Keeper of the Records and the real mastermind behind the alternate timeline's creation. The second surprise was Ruth's plan itself. She had advised Gregory to revisit notable events within his own lifetime and wait for Emmett to find him, as Emmett continues to recruit rebel Time Travelers for his own purposes. The third surprise was Gregory's announcement to a number of us at the banquet that he had, in fact, discovered the location of Emmett's alternate timeline—timeline CIV—where he had apparently visited an alternate League facility just like our own.

Before we had determined what might be the best course of action in this business of interfering with Emmett's plans for an alternate timeline, Milton #71 (our ATL Mission Supervisor) frantically entered the banquet room and alarmed us all with the declaration that "Emma #119 has been taken!"

To be sure, it goes without saying that I am unaware of anyone within the League School, or upon the governing Core itself, who is fond of Emma #119, or her severe-looking, black, horned-rim spectacles. In spite of her longstanding employment within the League, she is truly a disagreeable figure and without doubt the most critical personality among us. Nonetheless, she is part of this work, a member of the time-traveling vocation, and is, therefore, one of us. As such, we must endeavor to set aside this quandary as to why Emmett might desire her presence in the first place and do all that we can to find her.

It was that very motivation that prompted me to bid farewell to my sweetheart (and most frequent roommate) Athena with an embrace and a brief kiss. Shortly thereafter, George and I gathered with the other graduates and members of the Core for our collective departure from the League facility to timeline CIV. In addition to Gregory #143, we were joined by three members of the governing Core: ATL Mission Supervisor, Milton #71; Hakim #60, the tallest and gentlest ebony-colored man I have ever had the privilege to know; and Ruth #7, the author of our text and the one individual who knows the rebel Emmett best of all.

Such was the course of events for all that was to follow.

As is always the case in these time-traveling expeditions, I took my Horologium timepiece in hand and moved the hands of the watch in the appropriate direction. I next gave thought to the very situation and location that Gregory had just described for us and softly repeated aloud several times over "League facility timeline CIV." Although my eyes remained closed, I could hear my travel companions mumbling the very same words to themselves. I next moved my thumb to press the "TEMPUS" button within the watch's facing, took a deep breath, and immediately possessed the awareness that I was beginning to fall.

It goes without saying that my life has often been driven by curiosity. For that very reason, I have frequently given conjecture to the very nature of this "fall." I have considered whether it might somehow be the only means of travel between two points in time. I have reflected upon the possibility that it could be connected to topics Agnes #23 has only briefly discussed within our curriculum (and I have yet to fully comprehend) such as "dimensional shifts" and "intra-universe wormholes." Of late, however, I have given serious consideration to the possibility that this fall is nothing more than a movement in consciousness — a journey of one's perception between two points contained within space-time.

In any event, although I had certainly opened my eyes on previous journeys when more than one Time Traveler had been assigned to the same trip, I chose to open them again in an effort to see whether I could perceive any of the companions who accompanied me. As before, I saw no one falling but myself. In spite of the fact that these joint time-travel ventures inevitably entail arriving at one's destination together, the journey itself appears to be a truly solitary endeavor.

Much like the experience of a dream, I felt myself falling as if from an immense height to the ground located somewhere far below, as the wind rushed past my body and its extremities. In spite of my best efforts to breathe calmly, my heartbeat quickened, and the fall continued for some duration before suddenly coming to an immediate and abrupt halt. All at once, I found myself standing outside the doorway of what appeared to be an exact duplicate of the League Café—the very meeting place that Gregory #143 had proposed from the start.

I must acknowledge my immediate astonishment when we arrived at the café and my eyes gave witness to the fact that not a one among us appeared as the vaporous and ghostly forms that had here-to-for been a part of each of my previous time-traveling experiences. From the looks of astonishment upon the faces of my fellow classmates, it was clear that they were equally dumbfounded. I was about to inquire as to the nature of such a happening when Ruth #7 turned to speak, "The League facility exists outside of time—whether upon this timeline or upon the ATL." Her comment was matter of fact. As the statement provided no additional clarification as to the nature of such an event, I made a mental note to inquire further into the matter when the opportunity presented itself. All eyes next turned to Gregory, who was the reason we had arrived at such a location in the first place.

I have previously made note of the fact that I truly like Gregory. He is a man of complete integrity, and neither a braggart nor one prone to personal excess. During his life, he was a family man whose only other motivation was a focus on how best to be of service to others. For these reasons, I was never in favor of his eradication. To be sure, personal eradication remains the standard procedure prescribed by the League Disciplinary Process for anyone who has committed four or more offenses against time-travel protocols. However, dealing with all those who have abandoned the League in the selfsame manner without taking into account the rationale behind such an action is, without doubt, a most erroneous and mistaken policy. These very thoughts crossed my mind just as Ruth #7 looked to him with a query.

"Has Emmett recreated the entire League facility?" After glancing toward the café and its various tables, she turned to peer down the long hallway. No one besides our group of travelers seemed to be present. Ruth looked back in his direction.

"He has," came Gregory's first response, before adding, "As you know, my stay here was brief. During that time, I most often ventured between the library, the League Café, and the administrative offices but everything seems to be an exact replica of the League headquarters."

For a moment, each of us appeared to ponder some aspect of the situation before us. Milton #71's English accent finally broke the silence, "Where did you last see Emmett?"

Gregory nodded, "When I was here, Emmett spent most of his time in the library or in the administrative offices."

Hakim #60 was quick to interject, "How many others are with him?" Although gentle in manner, he towered more than a head above the rest of us.

Gregory continued, "In the beginning, I saw only Emmett and the former instructor, Bruce. Toward the end, I encountered Sybil, who came after my arrival."

"So, he found her?" Ruth pondered aloud.

My French classmate, Bonne Soeur Marie, volunteered, "But what of Emma #119?"

Gregory shook his head, "I never saw her."

Soeur Marie looked among us and inquired further, "What does this mean?"

It was Ruth #7 who replied, "I don't know yet."

In the end, it was decided that we should separate into two groups as our best means of finding Emmett, as he and his few companions appeared to pose little threat to our group of nine. Bonne Soeur Marie, Ruth, Emanuel #41, Gregory, and I would travel in the direction of the immense Akasha library—the very place Emmett had spent most of his time when he worked among us. For their part, Milton, George, Hakim, and Manuela would journey toward the administrative offices and look for him there.

Ruth led the way as we traveled down one corridor after another, taking the lengthy journey toward the library. I walked next to my classmate, Emanuel, who suddenly spoke the very idea that had come into my mind.

He pondered aloud, "I well remember my surprise at the enormity of this facility when Agnes first led us to the library depository."

I chuckled, "After that first trip, I had to get a copy of Agnes's 'officially approved League student handout' for its illustrative map of the route."

"After so many excursions to the place, I could draw the map from memory," he replied.

"Me, as well."

Ruth #7 led our group down one corridor after another. We took the familiar turn into one hallway and then proceeded toward another. The whole while I found myself amazed by the exact duplication of all that I could see before me. Save for the fact that we had yet to encounter anyone else, the alternate facility appeared to be a replica of our own upon the ATL. After several additional turns and traveling through a number of long passageways, we finally stood before the library's enormous double doorway.

"We're here," I said aloud.

Ruth turned to us. Her sparkling eyes appeared filled with caution, "We do not know whether Emmett is beyond this doorway, or whether Bruce or Sybil or anyone else may be waiting for us. For your own safety, do not venture further than your ability to see at least one of us at all times. Understood?"

The four of us immediately nodded in agreement, submitting to her words. Although Ruth chose the appearance of a 20-year-old in the prime of life, she was a League elder and perhaps the wisest of us all.

Bonne Soeur Marie took hold of the handle of one of the enormous doors, turned to Ruth, and inquired, "Maintenant . . . Now?"

Ruth nodded. Soeur Marie opened the doorway, and we five quickly proceeded inside the immense Akasha chamber.

Just as in the real Akasha library back at the League facility, there were books as far as one could see— thousands of books, hundreds of thousands. The countless volumes had been neatly organized on shelves that towered several stories above the ground. Ruth led us toward the central open space within the chamber that served as a reception area with a few tables and chairs. From this vantage point, the vast stacks of shelves fanned out in many directions. Each of us took turns peering down one corridor of books after another, looking for anyone else who might be present. From the start, we saw no one.

As it appeared safe, we began to expand the distances between us—although remaining cognizant of the need to perceive at least one of our fellow travelers at all times.

I followed the signage toward the "things that might have been" corridor of books and took turns glancing between Ruth (who stood at the entrance of the "things that may be still" section) and Bonne Soeur Marie (who stood near the "things that should be" section—the approved timeline). I could no longer see Emanuel, as he had journeyed down the corridor where Soeur Marie was already standing. Gregory had traveled in the same direction, as well.

We spent a great deal of time walking through one section of the Akasha after another, all the while managing to keep an eye out for each other. In such a fashion, we covered much of the chamber and journeyed away from the central-most point to explore a goodly number of the specialized collections in the enormous rooms beyond. Finally, after occupying ourselves for more than an hour, I heard Hakim's voice towering over my head.

"We found no one in any of the administrative offices."

I spun around to see him and Manuela standing beside me. Shortly thereafter, eight of us chose to journey back to the central chamber, waiting only on Emanuel. He followed a slight distance behind, carrying three enormous books that he placed on the library table before us.

After setting down the texts, he stated mysteriously, "I find what I am about to show you both interesting and quite confusing."

He opened the first volume and pointed to the page before us. It was blank. There was absolutely nothing written on it. Nothing at all. It was only a piece of white paper that had been bound along with the others. He turned the pages within the tome to show how each of them was blank, as well. He turned to the second book and showed us that, once again, there was nothing within its many pages but blank, white paper. The third volume proved to be exactly the same.

His words were filled with surprise, "They all look like this."

It was Manuela #64 who inquired, "If this is an alternate timeline to our own, why are the books empty?"

Milton and Ruth looked at each other, but it was Ruth who spoke, "Because this is not Emmett's real alternate. This is nothing more than a decoy." She was quiet for a few moments before adding, "It would appear that Emmett has been creating more than one timeline in order to complicate our efforts to stop him."

As soon as we returned to the actual League Café upon the ATL, rather than having the opportunity to discuss amongst ourselves what was to come next in our collective search to find Emmett and his rebels, we were suddenly greeted with the blaring sound of the alarm system ringing throughout the entire facility.

"You have got to be kidding!" George shouted with irritation.

The buzzer's noise was so loud it made any attempt at normal conversation impossible. As the incessant ringing continued, our group split up with Ruth leading three others toward the administrative offices. We five Wayfarer graduates walked dutifully down the corridor toward our old classroom doorway—just as we had done on countless occasions. Emanuel was in the lead, followed by George and me; Manuela and Bonne Soeur Marie were close behind.

When we arrived at the classroom, it was no surprise to find Agnes #23 pacing before her whiteboard and desk, shaking her head in dismay. In one hand she gripped the ever-present stylus. In the other, she held two pieces of paper—undoubtedly, the emergency assignment from the ATL Mission Office. The blare of the alarm continued for a time, only abating after we had all taken a seat. When the buzzing finally ceased, Agnes bobbed about, waving her stylus before us.

"We have an emergency assignment!" she said, pointing her stylus at each of us in turn. "A lesser timeline is exerting prominence and threatens the entire ATL! The matter is so complicated that even the ATL Mission Office is uncertain what our best course of action might be. I need some options, and I need them now!" She stood silent as if awaiting a response.

Bonne Soeur Marie was quick to interject, "Madame, surely we must know the problem if we are expected to recommend a solution."

I knew George intended to annoy our instructress when he stated, "Perhaps we should have some additional background on the topic? We always benefit from your background information."

Agnes looked at him with irritation, slapped her desk with the same fist holding the mission assignment, and responded, "I will tell you what caused the problem!" She turned to write a three-word phrase on the whiteboard before us, "Death of Olympias," underlining each of the words twice over for emphasis.

The phrase before me caused me to catch my breath. Agnes turned in my direction and inquired, "Ben, do you remember your encounter with Emmett on timeline CCCIV?"

"I do," was all that would come to me.

Agnes #23 frowned and waved the mission

assignment pages in my direction, "Would you like to remind everyone else?"

Within but a moment I had gathered my thoughts and proceeded, "As you no doubt recall, after Elder Professor Grimwald #94 had compiled his listing of the 2,857 timelines upon which Emmett could be hiding, I journeyed to timeline CCCIV and found myself witness, yet again, to the very banquet at which Alexander the Great had contracted Guillain-Barré. I stood as a silent observer, watching the emperor chewing morsels of gizzards and onions when the ghostly forms of Emmett and Bruce appeared before me. A few moments later, Emmett instructed Bruce to journey back in time, where he influenced one of Olympias's attendants to arrange for her death . . ."

Agnes interrupted impatiently, "Just remind us, what happened!"

"Olympias was Alexander's mother. She is rumored to have been involved in the assassination of Alexander's father, Phillip—an act that put her son on the throne. Since she died, Alexander was never born on that timeline, and his father, Phillip, remained King of Macedonia. Because Alexander did not exist, Persia was never conquered, and Darius remained ruler of the Persian Empire. While I was there, I watched and stood witness as the form of Alexander suddenly disappeared, only to be replaced by Emperor Darius instead."

"Exactly!" Agnes slapped her desk with her fist again, while adding, "And that is the problem!"

My sometimes roomie, George, responded, "Excuse me, but I am still somewhat unclear as to the exact nature of the problem before us."

Agnes whipped around, pointing her stylus in his direction, "The problem is that Darius now aligns with Rome, and the two former rivals became allies in their quest to conquer Greece. After that, the Roman Empire moves westward toward Europe and then England. Persia moves east to conquer India and then China. These changes will impact civilization for hundreds of years to come. That is why the alarm has sounded."

Manuela #64 pondered aloud, "So a minor timeline has somehow moved toward prominence?"

"Exactly!" Agnes repeated herself. "And I need some options!"

Soeur Marie was the first to volunteer, "We could go back and save Olympias," prompting Agnes to write the words (with appropriate underlines) "Save Olympias" on the board.

"We could," Agnes admitted, "and that may be the best course of action, but it creates a new problem." She bounced about, appearing to wait for a response.

Finally, Bonne Soeur Marie spoke, "Quel problème . . . what problem?"

I chose to reply, "If I am standing next to Emmett and the two of us are watching Alexander, and Alexander fails to disappear after Bruce goes back to alter the timeline, Emmett will immediately know that the League has interfered." I paused for only a moment before adding, "Emmett was Keeper of the Records for a very long time. In spite of what he told me, he had to know that this would cause a major disruption to the timeline. He wanted to keep us occupied. Even if we decide to save Olympias, Emmett can simply go back and influence the timeline again."

"It is still an option," George said aloud. "Perhaps Emmett needs to stop underestimating the rest of us."

Agnes was noticeably frustrated, "It's on the board! I need another option."

Manuela #64 voiced her thoughts aloud, "What if we altered the timeline much later and undermined either Persia or Rome? Alexander would still disappear during your encounter, and for a time Emmett would believe his plans had not changed. Did Rome or Persia ever have an enemy that nearly defeated them?"

Our scholarly Swede was quick to respond, "As I recall, Rome feared Hannibal, who came closest to conquering them."

Manuela continued, "Why did he not succeed?"

As was often the case, Emanuel had an answer, "Because his own city of Carthage had grown weary of war and refused to fund his army or supply additional troops for any further conflict. The city's leaders were hopeful that Hannibal would succeed in his conquest without having to incur any inconvenience on their part."

Agnes nodded and wrote the words "Influence Carthage" on the board, underlined them, and then inquired, "And is there a problem?"

Emanuel volunteered a challenge to the solution he had just provided, "There may be too many unknowns. Unless the Akasha has noted other timelines in which such occurred, we can't possibly know the outcomes we will face by creating this is kind of interference. Carthage taking over the Roman Empire may present a new set of challenges to history. We could ask Athena to look into the matter, but if it is an unknown, the risk may be greater than any reward."

Agnes nodded, "Athena knows everything!" and then inquired, "Do we have any other options?"

My next comment came across somewhat nonchalant, "We could wait until Emmett thinks he has succeeded and then go back and kill Phillip, Alexander's father."

"What?" George was quick to respond, "How can you suggest such a thing?"

I remained detached, "George, he dies on the ATL anyway, and we know what happens to Greece when Alexander dies — the empire is fractured by his generals into three separate nations. Perhaps three sovereignties warring against Rome and Persia will diminish the influence of the timeline back to its lesser significance?"

Agnes turned to the board and wrote, "Kill Phillip," just as Emanuel voiced aloud, "Although I am personally opposed to such an idea, from the League's perspective such a solution may create the lesser of all problems."

"I will ask Athena," came my reply.

Agnes nodded and repeated, "Athena knows everything . . ."

We five Wayfarer graduates stood in the centermost chamber of the Akasha library, as my Mediterranean sweetheart, Athena, spoke, pointing to several of the enormous volumes on the tabletop before her, "According to the records, if your ultimate goal is to influence timeline CCCIV back to diminished prominence, then the best approach is probably to eliminate Alexander's father, Phillip II . . ."

George shook his head in frustration, prompting Athena to add, "I know how you feel about allowing this kind of thing, George, but I have looked at nearly twenty of the most prominent timelines, and every one of them points to the very same outcome — the division of Macedonia creates decades of challenges for Greece, as well as the Roman and Persian Empires. The supremacy of the approved timeline needs to remain intact. This is the best approach."

Athena unconsciously twirled a few strands of hair

between her fingertips as she looked between us. I could not help but smile when she turned in my direction. As had occurred on so many previous occasions, I was frequently amazed that such an incredible woman had chosen to love me. Athena continued to watch each of us, awaiting further comment or query.

Finally, Manuela #64 broke the silence, "Any suggestion as to how it might be done?"

Athena nodded and pointed at one of the books before us, "Honestly, it is remarkable that Phillip lived as long as he did. Over the years, he had a number of battle injuries that would have killed lesser men . . ."

Soeur Marie interrupted, "Comme quoi . . . like what?"

Athena continued, "On one occasion, an arrow pierced and embedded itself in his right eye. Both the eye and the arrow were removed, but the injury scarred the right socket and permanently disfigured his face."

I grimaced at the thought of both the arrow and its removal, as Athena continued, "During one battle, he fractured his collarbone and right arm when his horse was killed beneath him, and the two tumbled to the ground. He probably came closest to death during another encounter when a lance pierced his left leg, destroyed his knee, embedded itself in the bone, and fractured a one-inch hole in his tibia. The lance was removed and the hole in his leg and bone was stuffed with cloth-soaked vinegar, which was a common treatment back then."

I grimaced a second time as she finished, "The injury left him barely able to walk."

Emanuel pondered aloud, "For Phillip to survive such injuries, his physicians must have been quite skilled for the era."

"They were," Athena conceded. "The most notable of which was Cristobulus, trained in the methods of Hippocrates."

Finally, my occasional roomie, George, noted, "It's surprising that he didn't succumb to an infection from either the arrow or the lance."

Athena pointed back toward the volumes, "I thought the same thing myself, but it appears both weapons were clean when they struck him."

Suddenly, Bonne Soeur Marie turned to us and responded, "Je comprend . . . I understand. I know what to do."

It may be surprising to consider that even before your Wayfarer graduation — truly prior to your recruitment into the League — you became a participant in countless experiences of personal time travel. The very same has occurred for all conscious beings within the third-dimensional plane. Such a statement may give rise to reflection, bewilderment, and even disagreement but its validity remains beyond question.

Close your eyes and reflect upon some happening in your life — an important event, a noteworthy encounter, a first love, the birth of a child, the death of someone you hold dear. Imagine all that occurred within that single moment of time. Bring to mind the images, the sounds, and the sensations of everything around you. When you have truly recalled this incident in your mind, you have moved to that very episode in your life's journey. Should you contend that such an occurrence is nothing more than a movement in consciousness, consider the following, "How truly different is this from the ongoing experience of a Wayfarer Time Traveler?"

Excerpt, "Understanding the Nature of Time Travel," *Wayfarer's Manual — Continuing Education (revised edition);* **by Ruth #7**

TWO: *Journal Entry — December 11 ATL*

Once again, I found myself called to Meeting Room 2, near the administrative offices, for a discussion with members of the Core. Milton #71 and Ruth #7 sat on one side of the table, across from the Governor-General, Sara #11, and me. Sara had sent a message with a simple forewarning, "We need to meet about Emmett."

The Governor-General looked briefly toward Ruth and Milton before turning back in my direction, "Ben, based on the group's recent experience with the duplicate facility on timeline CIV, I thought it might be best if we gathered to hear again everything you can remember from any of your conversations with Emmett after he left the League . . ."

I was quick to respond, "I am certain that I have already told you everything."

"I understand," Sara nodded, "but it might be helpful. We need to see if we can discover what he is really doing."

Ruth came next, the youthfulness of her eyes glistened as she spoke, "Ben, timeline CIV was a decoy, not a duplicate. We need to better understand what Emmett is up to. For whatever reason, while he was here, he felt closest to you. Perhaps he said something to you during one of your encounters that might give us a glimpse into his plans."

"Yes, Chap," Milton agreed, "just start at the beginning. Tell us anything you can recall — anything at all."

Having long been a champion of collaboration in any endeavor, I was quick to agree and reflected aloud all that I could remember, beginning with, "I have seen Emmett on three occasions since his departure. During the first, he did not see me, nor did he become aware of my presence." I turned toward the Governor-General and then reminded the others, "During that mission, Sara loaned me her Horologium so that I would remain unseen. I stood witness, yet again, to Alexander's banquet. All at once, Emmett and a much shorter man, whom I discovered to be Bruce, suddenly appeared before me."

I paused momentarily, looking at Sara to confirm she recalled the story, as I had related it previously. She only motioned for me to proceed, "Go on."

I continued, "Bruce seemed frustrated with Emmett. He said that the two of them should be focusing on the duplicate ATL. I remember he told Emmett, 'The approach you have chosen means there is much more that needs to be done.'"

"What did Emmett say in response?" came Ruth's inquiry.

"He said that they were ensuring the outcome and that it was best not to underestimate the Governor-General herself or Milton's knowledge of history. In the end, he told Bruce that what they were doing was nothing more than a diversion."

Ruth pondered aloud, "So he specifically mentioned Milton and Sara . . . ?"

Milton interrupted, "It would appear that describing it as a diversion fits timeline CIV perfectly."

Sara inquired, "Anything else?"

"No, that was my first encounter."

"And the second, my good man?" Milton asked.

I nodded, "It was during my mission to assist the African ruler Keita – the one who created the Manden Charter, which is an oral tradition that champions peace, human rights, personal security, and self-expression."

"I am quite familiar with Keita and his charter," came Milton's response.

"During that assignment, I found myself somewhat startled when Emmett appeared before me." I sighed, "I must admit that I was surprised to see him and immediately asked, 'How did you know where to find me?' He said only that he had looked into the Akasha to see my upcoming missions, and this was one of them . . ."

Sara appeared shocked and she turned to Ruth, "Is that even possible?"

Ruth pondered the question for a moment before adding, "Not as simply as Emmett described. Every choice and interaction has an impact on a timeline. For that reason, seeing such a consequence would only become possible when Ben was assigned the mission. At that point, the outcome in alignment with the approved timeline and 'things that should be' would become visible to the Akasha."

I waited until she had finished before continuing, "Emmett insisted that the League's approach to fixing timelines was a never-ending process and that we were all wasting our time." I concluded with the statement, "Emmett invited me to come and work with him."

"Anything else?" Sara asked for a second time.

I began, "I don't think . . ." and then added quickly, "Wait, that was when Emmett told me he would check in on me again. I remember him saying, 'I was most intrigued by what happened on your Eleanor Roosevelt mission.' He said something about it being the first time he had ever witnessed such an occurrence."

The Governor-General appeared surprised when she stated aloud, "That is your next mission."

Ruth added, "And Emmett told you this before you had been given the assignment at the commencement ceremony?"

"Yes."

Ruth turned to Milton, "When were those assignments chosen?"

Milton responded immediately, "I worked on pulling them together with Louise #217 that very morning."

"How is that possible?" the Governor-General inquired.

Ruth was obviously startled, "It's not. Seeing this kind of outcome before the mission was even assigned would not be possible by simply looking at the Akasha." She added, "Truly, this is most interesting. I need to look into this further."

Sara inquired, "How are you going to do that?"
Ruth pondered the query before adding, "I think I have an idea," although she said no more.

There was only silence until Sara spoke again, "Tell us about your third encounter, Ben."

"On that occasion, Emmett asked Bruce to go back and eliminate Olympias from the timeline. Remember? In the midst of that encounter, Emmett told me he had ways of knowing what the League was doing. He even knew about Elder Professor Grimwald's 2,857 timelines where we had begun searching for Emmett and his rebels."

Sara spoke again, "I am assuming that members of the Core are still looking into whether we might have someone within the facility passing information on to Emmett?"

Milton replied, "Most assuredly. I am overseeing the matter myself."

Sara turned next to me and then looked toward Milton, "Has the issue of Olympias's death been addressed to diminish the prominence of the timeline?"

Milton replied again, "Most assuredly. Phillip was killed upon the timeline, prompting his kingdom to fracture. The timeline has returned to lesser significance. Ben, do tell them how it was rectified."

I nodded, "Bonne Soeur Marie went back and influenced the gladiator whose spear had punctured a hole in Phillip's leg. Apparently, there is an old Greek insult that suggests someone is fond of eating dung . . ."

"Kópros," Milton interrupted.

"Exactly," I continued, "Soeur Marie influenced the gladiator to thoroughly cover the end of his lance with horse manure as he shouted that statement and hurled it in Phillip's direction."

Sara and Ruth turned inquisitively to Milton who replied only, "Death by bacterial infection."

⧗ ⧗ ⧗

Setting aside both the uncertainty of dealing with Emmett's alternate timeline as well as my forthcoming mission to interact with one Eleanor Roosevelt, I purposefully chose instead to schedule private time with my beloved in her chambers. It took a few minutes to convince her to do likewise, as her own agenda was scheduled with numerous research projects detailing the various potentials and preferred outcomes for each of my colleague's mission assignments.

We lay side by side within the bedsheet that had become entangled between us. I stared for a moment at the intensity of her beautiful brown eyes and then moved to kiss her once again upon the lips.

She smiled back at me, "You know you're interfering with my work schedule, don't you?"

I replied only, "Never leave for tomorrow what can be accomplished today."

Athena looked at me curiously, taking a strand of her hair between her fingertips, and inquired as she twirled it, "Do you mean my work, or us here shaking the sheets?"

"Both."

She smiled, "Well, we have finally had our time together, but I still have my work."

"You are responsible for too many mission assignments."

"It's getting better," came her reply, "Louise #217 has started to become quite helpful."

Knowing the subject of Louise remained fraught with large measures of rivalry and jealousy between us, I mumbled only, "Mmmm."

Athena inquired, "When are you leaving?"

A look of perplexity crossed my face, "From here?"

"No!" she nudged me with her hand, "When are you leaving for the Eleanor Roosevelt assignment?"

I nodded, "I will be leaving sometime today. George and I are meeting in the library for some last-minute research." I sighed and spoke aloud, "I just can't help but wonder how Emmett even knew I was going there before the trip had been assigned. Ruth said she was going to investigate further how such a thing was possible."

"It is most curious," she said, continuing to twirl her hair. In the next moment, her eyes opened with surprise as she exclaimed, "I have a thought."

"Pray tell," I responded.

"What if Emmett saw you there because he was there at the same time? Perhaps he simply encountered you during your own mission?"

I considered her statement and then pondered aloud, "You mean, Emmett has already gone back and stood witness to a mission that I have yet to undertake?"

"Yes, remember you mentioned that he said he was 'intrigued' and had 'never before witnessed such an occurrence.' Maybe he witnessed it because he was there. It hasn't happened for you yet, but it has already happened for him."

"That would certainly explain things." I smiled, leaned forward, and kissed her again, "You really are most amazing."

Athena smiled back, but in the next instant her expression changed to one of deep concern, "Let's hope he is there," she said finally, "because if he is not, whatever Emmett is doing with his timeline may be much more complicated than any of us have imagined."

George and I had been studiously researching our respective missions for well over an hour. We sat at one of the library tables with several volumes of books scattered between us. For much of that time, words did not pass between us, save for an occasional sigh or a sound of surprise uttered by one or the other as we happened upon some unusual piece of information. To be sure, these faint sounds never rose to a level that prompted a query from the other, as our personal thoughts remained our own. It was a long while before George finally cleared his throat, delivering a question out of nowhere.

"Do you have any recollection as to how many individuals succumbed to the pox?"

Uncertain that I had heard his exact query, I looked up from the text before me, "What?"

George began anew, "In the colonies, do you remember how many died from smallpox?"

As the subject was well-known to me, I nodded and replied, "The count exceeded 150,000 souls."

My sometimes-roomie appeared somber, "More than a million died from this coronavirus." When I looked at him inquisitively, he added, "In the States alone . . . more than a million died from the coronavirus."

"I am surprised that such a matter has been assigned to you." I pondered aloud, "Wouldn't Bonne Soeur Marie #304 and her curative measures be better suited for such an endeavor?"

He shook his head in the negative, "Perhaps in the States, but I am headed for the Philippines. My target is truly an amazing woman—Tessie Sy-Coson. Much like myself, she possesses a background in business and philanthropy."

I was perplexed, "How does philanthropy deal with a virus?"

George described his target with some measure of pride, "This woman is formidable and forward-thinking. As soon as this coronavirus made its appearance, she convinced her company to inoculate all 120,000 of its employees and then provided inoculations for government staff and the underprivileged. She also directed the company to donate millions in equipment to those involved in healthcare so that they could adequately fight the problem." He nodded approvingly. "She is most fond of the motto 'people helping people.'"

"Tessie sounds like your kind of woman, George." I smiled, ". . . the kind that might make Louise jealous."

George appeared confused, "What are you talking about?"

I shook my head, "Have you yet to realize that Louise is infatuated with you?"

He frowned, "If Louise has any interest in me, it is only because she cannot have you."

I quickly changed the topic, returning our focus to the mission at hand, "What is the purpose of your assignment?"

"On multiple timelines, members of Tessie's board were never enthused about the company's involvement with an unknown virus of undetermined duration. My job is simply to influence them and ensure that Tessie wins out." George was silent for only a moment before inquiring, "What about this Roosevelt woman?"

"She is most formidable, as well."

George waved his hand in my direction, "Tell me."

"She maintains a schedule of activities that few could hope to equal." I pointed to one of the texts before me, "As you know, I am quite fond of writing, but this woman is truly prodigious. Aside from daily letters – many of which exceed ten pages or more – for nearly forty years, she wrote a column for newspapers six days a week! In the midst of the Depression, she visited every state in the union so that the government might discover how best to be of assistance to the people. According to the ATL, in the midst of a world at war, she is destined to travel to six continents and dozens of countries – speaking to hundreds of thousands of soldiers. She will inspire countless individuals, even in the face of war, adversity, and lack. In spite of harsh criticism for doing so, she will argue against all manner of prejudice and became a defender of women's rights, what they call 'civil rights,' the rights of refugees, the poor, and the underprivileged. As First Lady, she puts duty and country above all else and is instrumental in her husband's role as President. In spite of condemnation throughout much of her life, the approved timeline suggests that she is to become one of the most influential women of the 20th century."

"What is your assignment?"

"I am traveling to a time early in the war. She needs some encouragement to become a champion for individuals around the world and set aside her desire to retire . . . The ATL shows her as instrumental in drafting a Universal Declaration of Human Rights."

George was impressed, "Truly, such a woman must be proud of so many accomplishments?"

I shook my head, "On the contrary. She does not think highly of herself, her accomplishments, or her abilities. She has never considered herself either a good wife or a good mother and has long maintained a belief that she is altogether unattractive. She has long possessed a crippling fear of public speaking. To be sure, she thinks herself ill-suited for many things, and often feels unequipped for much that lays before her."

"Then how does she manage to accomplish so much?"

I looked at him intensely, "She lives by a motto of her own." I pointed at her own words contained within the text before me, "'You must do the things you think you cannot do.'"

After an extremely rapid descent (that is always customary on these time-travel excursions), I suddenly found myself within the body of one Anna Eleanor Roosevelt—henceforth, Eleanor, First Lady of these United States. I saw the vaporous forms of my hands and arms envelop her own extremities as she walked down the lengthy hallway. I could hear the sounds of her footsteps clicking against the wooden floorboards that appeared every few feet between the lengths of old carpeting that had been placed within the passageway. I noted how the walls had been adorned with portraits of various sizes—only a few of whose faces appeared known to me—and how the hallway was scattered with many more chairs than seemed necessary for such a corridor.

Once these reflections had passed through my mind, I felt the thoughts of the First Lady push them aside and take their place. She was determined to oversee the arrangements for "the visitor" (or visitors, as Franklin had been entirely unclear on that point). At first, she had been somewhat dismayed by the announcement that they would be hosting a surprise visitor over Christmastide—in addition to everything else slated for their schedules! Franklin had been quite firm in his refusal to provide additional information, but it was wartime and security was understandably a cause for concern. Still, it did not make easy any of the preparations that needed to occur beforehand. Franklin's instructions had been simply, "Babs, we will be having a guest stay over through Christmas. In all likelihood, more than one. They may be here well into the New Year."

"How many are we expecting?" Eleanor had inquired.

"Can't say how many," Franklin replied, "I would expect three or more." He paused and then quickly added, "I would suggest we have on hand plenty of scotch, whiskey, brandy, and a quantity of some very good champagne."

I muttered to myself, "Sounds like they're tipplers," as Eleanor continued on her way. She gave thought to various considerations as to the sleeping arrangements and then decided the main guest would be most comfortable in the Rose Bedroom, as such a visitor would no doubt be traveling with sufficient luggage for an extended stay and the room offered enormous closets and a very nice bath. The rest of the entourage would be given an appropriate number of the smaller bedrooms. These decisions prompted her to sigh with relief at having completed at least something on her ever-present checklist.

Having inhabited the thoughts of multiple heads of state, I was certainly accustomed to the many deliberations that passed through the minds of such individuals. Eleanor was no different. As she turned to walk down the stairway to the first floor, her list of most pressing activities fluttered before me. There was her column to write. She had a radio address later that afternoon. She was long overdue on a letter to someone named "Hick." There were several tasks awaiting her presence at the Civil Defense office. She had innumerable parties at which she had to make an appearance, including three sponsored by the

Washington Federation of Churches. In addition to a never-ending stack of mail and correspondence that had to be addressed, she had several talks that still needed to be worked on. The list went on and on. Although it had eased their schedules somewhat, she remained mournful that this Christmas would be the first without the children. Their sons – James, Elliott, Franklin Jr., and John – were all on active duty, and Anna and her husband had relocated to Seattle. All these thoughts passed before me.

When she took the final step to the first floor, she sighed again, recalling the rejuvenation and quiet that was hers at Val-Kill Cottage. In spite of the present demands on her time, she was certain she would get to enjoy her retirement there one day. She had already remodeled the cottage in 1936, thinking retirement would be hers at the end of Franklin's second term. Unfortunately, both the Depression and world events had prompted him to seek re-election and an unprecedented third time. Truly, one of her primary roles was to pass on to Franklin issues of importance, so duty had come before desire. She had no choice but to continue on. Still, she had every intention of returning to Val-Kill, just as soon as it was practical.

In the midst of such thoughts, I managed to separate my consciousness from that of the First Lady and looked down at my own legs as they stepped forth from her body. My ghostly form continued to walk in waves of swirling motion next to Eleanor. Suddenly, the sounds of commotion followed by a deep voice came to our ears. We both turned in the direction of the main entryway where we could see (and smell) great wafts of cigar smoke filling the air as a roundish, cherub-faced man ambled quickly toward us.

As I turned, for a brief instant I saw the ghostly form of Ruth #7 standing as witness off in the distance. Her vaporous body moved as a transparent ghost as she looked first to Churchill, then Eleanor, and then to me. A moment later she was gone, and I heard the low, raspy voice of an Englishman speak the words, "Mrs. Roosevelt, thank you for having me." Eleanor replied in response, "Mr. Churchill, so you are our surprise visitor."

Having long been an advocate of hard work and self-discipline, I found myself truly inspired by the efforts of the First Lady, the President, and the Prime Minister, Mr. Churchill. To take note of all that I witnessed among these three throughout the days that followed would present an exhaustive tome. For that reason, I choose instead to present here a mere highlight of my observations.

I have already made note of portions of Eleanor's schedule. To be sure, both the President and the Prime Minister maintained a similar level of activities. That first evening, there was a welcome party to honor Mr. Churchill and his entourage, which included several diplomatic, military, and Scotland Yard personnel. Cocktails followed at 8:15, with dinner for seventeen guests hosted by the First Lady a half hour later. After dinner and brandy, the Prime Minister and the British Ambassador met with the President, the Secretary of State, and several others until half past midnight to discuss Allied plans for the war. I noticed early on that in spite of being wheelchair-bound, such inconvenience did not appear to interfere with the President's activities in the least.

The next morning, Roosevelt, Churchill, and several others gathered to meet on the topic of "Foreign

Relations of the United States." After lunch, the President was engaged in various meetings dealing with Senators, senior staff, and issues of import, while Churchill took a nap. (I came to discover that a daily nap was a customary ritual for the Prime Minister.) At 4:00 p.m. that afternoon, both the President and the Prime Minister held – what was called – "a joint press conference" with a large number of reporters gathering for the occasion. The press conference was followed by another meeting whose sole focus was "the transportation of supplies and equipment." Dinner that evening consisted of eleven guests, again hosted by Eleanor, and included Secretary of Commerce, Harry Hopkins, who remained present for a private meeting, which followed at midnight.

The next day, after a series of meetings for each of the three, the First Lady played host to the Crown Prince and Princess of Norway (and their children), followed by a late afternoon party for all concerned, and then radio addresses by both Churchill and the President. President Roosevelt had to take time out for a previously scheduled doctor's appointment in the early afternoon but was back in time for the lighting of a National Christmas tree. A tea party at 5:45 p.m. gave way to cocktails at 7:45, followed by dinner at 8:30 for all those present.

Christmas Day, the next morning, included services at Foundry Methodist Church, attended by the President, the First Lady, the Prime Minister, all house guests, and various staff and security personnel. After services, nineteen guests returned for lunch, followed by a War Council meeting for the President, Churchill, and several Chiefs of Staff. Eleanor hosted a Christmas dinner that evening for sixty individuals, followed by carols, cocktails, and (what George had once described to me as) "a movie."

The day after Christmas, Winston Churchill addressed a joint meeting of Congress. In the days and weeks that followed, there would be even more meetings with Senators and Congressmen, as well as any number of assemblies with ambassadors, diplomats, and heads of state from many different countries – Argentina, Australia, Bolivia, Canada, Costa Rica, Denmark, El Salvador, Honduras, Iceland, India, Mexico, Panama, Poland, the Netherlands, Nicaragua, Norway, Poland, South Africa, the Soviet Union, Uruguay, Venezuela – the listing proved to be a vast composition that the President referred to as "the Allied powers."

I must admit two thoughts frequently came to mind during all this hubbub of activity. The first was that I had yet to discover a circumstance to use my Wayfarer influence with Mrs. Roosevelt, and the second was that in spite of my remaining ever watchful for an appearance by Emmett, such an incident had yet to arise.

On several occasions, throughout the frenzied activity of those hectic days, Eleanor expressed concern for the toll they appeared to be taking on her husband. To be sure, the President was used to long hours on his own, but the Prime Minister was fond of working until 1 or 2 a.m., and Franklin felt obligated to stay up with him in order to discuss any number of subjects related to the war. All of this was on top of his own schedule, without having the benefit of one of Mr. Churchill's daily rejuvenation naps.

I came to believe the Prime Minister's daily naps were, in part, a consequence of his drinking. While still in his bedclothes, Churchill began each day with a scotch and soda, followed by another glass of the same every hour until lunchtime. Lunch was generally served with champagne followed by his regular nap. Upon arising, a glass of cognac passed through his lips, until the hourly scotch and soda resumed at four in the afternoon. Dinner was generally accompanied by sherry or something similar, with more champagne or wine served with the meal. The chosen beverage for the evening (lasting late until slumber) was brandy. Even amidst a routine such as this, the Prime Minister somehow managed to maintain his sense of mind and a robust schedule.

In any event, Eleanor had mentioned her concerns to Franklin – both in person and in a note, she had passed on to him through his secretary, Grace Tully. She was concerned that he was pushing himself too hard, but nothing had changed. For that reason, Eleanor planned to have lunch with the Prime Minister one afternoon while Franklin was elsewhere engaged. Her plan was simply to request that Churchill encourage the President to go to bed whenever he was tired – and certainly earlier than the current schedule. Still hoping to discern the best approach to my mission at hand, my vaporous self stood beside the Prime Minister as we awaited the arrival of the First Lady.

Winston was already seated at the table with an ashtray before him. In one hand, he held a thick cigar; the other grasped a glass of champagne – as noted, his most frequent beverage for lunchtime meals. Although he periodically glanced over his round spectacles at the newspaper on the tabletop before him, he seemed altogether focused on inhaling several drafts from the smokey cigar (followed by a generous gulp from the glass of champagne). When Eleanor entered the room, he placed his glass on the table. Still clutching the smoldering cigar, he rose to greet her.

"Mrs. Roosevelt," he said only.

"Mr. Prime Minister," came her response.

She motioned in the direction of the kitchen doorway for lunch to be served. I turned to see a cheerful Black butler nod in acknowledgment, and for a moment was quite certain that I perceived the ghostly form of Ruth #7 standing beside him. A moment later she was gone.

I began contemplating whether this was simply Ruth's attempt to further investigate the Emmett situation when Churchill's thoughts began to invade my own. Although he was definitely hungry, the Prime Minister had found the First Lady's frugality regarding most meals made for quite a difference with those served at 10 Downing Street. As they exchanged pleasantries, a lunch consisting of cold jellied bouillon, salmon salad, and – what appeared to be – bread and butter sandwiches was placed before them.

The Prime Minister's cigar smoldered in the ashtray as he took a spoon to the bouillon. After sampling a taste, he inquired, "Madame, do you know if someone was wandering the hallway last night – say about three in the morning?"

Eleanor looked up from her lunch and inquired, "Why do you ask, Mr. Churchill?"

The Prime Minister's words were slow and deliberate, "I could have sworn I heard footsteps outside my room." He peered over the top of his glasses, and stared directly into her eyes, "The night before, I was almost certain I heard a man's voice speaking to me."

Eleanor nodded for only a moment and then provided a reply that surprised even my vaporous self, "Perhaps you heard the White House ghost?"

Churchill appeared stunned, "I beg your pardon?"

"The White House is rumored to have a ghost . . ." she nodded again, "President Abraham Lincoln, to be exact."

The Prime Minister was astonished, "Madame, are you serious?"

"Yes, Mr. Churchill, I am quite serious." Eleanor took a small bite of her sandwich, chewed for a moment, and then added, "Several of the staff have reported either seeing or hearing Mr. Lincoln. Franklin has told me on two occasions that he heard someone speaking to him in the Oval Office, but no one was there . . . I have frequently witnessed Franklin's dog, Fala, bark at absolutely nothing at all in several of the White House rooms and hallways."

The Prime Minister peered over his oval lenses and inquired quite seriously, "Mrs. Roosevelt, have you ever seen President Lincoln yourself?"

Eleanor considered the query for several moments before responding, "No, Mr. Churchill, I have not seen him, but I am certain I have felt his presence." She said no more but instead took another bite from her sandwich.

"I see," came his reply. He took a puff from the cigar, momentarily contemplated her response, and then said, "Ambassador Halifax tells me you have had quite an impact on many people in this country through your travels and your talks."

She quickly changed the subject with her reply, "That is very kind of him to say . . . On another matter, I am wondering if I could speak to you for a moment about Franklin's schedule. He needs rest from some of these late-night meetings."

Winston placed his cigar in the ashtray and nodded agreeably, "Mrs. Roosevelt, please feel free to speak to me about anything."

As soon as the First Lady began to describe her concern about Franklin's late hours, my ghostly hand withdrew the Horologium timepiece from my pocket. I gave thought to revisiting the same conversation but a moment before. I used my Horologium accordingly and within the blink of an eye, I found that I had returned to the target of the First Lady as she replied, "No, Mr. Churchill, I have not seen him, but I am certain I have felt his presence," and took a bite of her sandwich.

"I see," came Churchill's reply. He held the cigar to his lips and appeared to consider the response before quickly moving on to other matters, "Ambassador Halifax tells me you have had quite an impact on many people in this country through your travels and your talks."

My second attempt proved no more fruitful than the first as Eleanor brushed the compliment aside, "That is most kind of him to say . . . On another matter, I am wondering if I could speak to you about Franklin's schedule. He needs rest from some of these late-night meetings."

Winston placed his cigar in the ashtray and nodded agreeably, "Mrs. Roosevelt, please feel free to speak to me about anything . . . anything at all."

As lunch continued and the First Lady described the toll that the late nights were having on her husband, I decided to take a more direct approach. For my third attempt, I chose to return to the start of their conversation. I proceeded to repeat, "Winston Churchill at lunch" several times over, pressed the TEMPUS button in the appropriate manner, and took a deep breath. Within an instant, I found myself back at the beginning of the engagement. To be sure, on this occasion it was apparent that things had changed ever so slightly.

I sat within Churchill's body, smelling the cigar smoke as it encircled my vaporous nostrils. He held the newspaper between his hands, with the cigar firmly clutched between his lips. A large snifter of brandy (instead of champagne) had been placed not too far distant from the ashtray. I silently whispered the words from Ruth's text, "Once interaction with a timeline has occurred, space-time is altered ever so slightly," just as the First Lady entered the room.

He folded the newspaper and placed it on the table. We rose to greet her, "Mrs. Roosevelt," he said.

"Mr. Prime Minister," she responded.

She signaled toward the butler. However, on this occasion, Ruth was nowhere to be seen. Pleasantries passed between the two of them as lunch was served. It appeared to be some type of consommé, a salad, and those ever-present bread and butter sandwiches.

After he had tasted the soup, Churchill inquired, "Madame, do you know if someone was wandering the hallway last night – say about three in the morning?"

"Why do you ask, Mr. Churchill?"

His voice was raspy, but the words were deliberate, "I could have sworn I heard footsteps outside my room." He peered over his glasses, enabling me to look right at the First Lady, "The night before, I was almost certain I heard a man's voice speaking to me."

Eleanor nodded and then stated, "Perhaps it was the White House ghost?"

Churchill was surprised, "I beg your pardon?"

"The White House is rumored to have a ghost . . . President Abraham Lincoln, to be exact."

The Prime Minister was stunned, "Madame, are you serious?"

"Yes, Mr. Churchill, I am quite serious." The First Lady took a bite of the sandwich before adding, "Several of the staff have reported either seeing or hearing Mr. Lincoln. Franklin has told me on two occasions that he heard someone speaking to him in the Oval Office, but no one was there . . . I have frequently witnessed Franklin's dog, Fala, bark at absolutely nothing at all . . ."

I felt the Prime Minister's skepticism, as he inquired, "Mrs. Roosevelt, have you ever seen President Lincoln yourself?"

Eleanor considered the query before responding, "No, Mr. Churchill, I have not seen him, but I believe I have felt his presence."

"I see," came his reply.

I closed my eyes and quickly gave thought to changing what he had said only a few minutes earlier. I focused my Wayfarer influence in that very direction and, once complete, I opened my eyes. All at once, it appeared that an idea had suddenly come to the forefront of the Prime Minister's mind. He drew another puff from his cigar and stated, "Ambassador Halifax tells me you have had quite an impact on many people in this country through your travels and your talks . . . I wonder if you would consider coming to England in order to assist us in the very same manner?"

She seemed surprised by the invitation, "I am not certain that I could do anything more than you yourself can accomplish."

The Prime Minister took a sip of brandy and seemed even more convinced of the worthiness of such an idea, "Mrs. Roosevelt, as you might imagine there are many pressing matters that occupy my time. You would be a great help to England, and to me."

"Wouldn't my visit be a hindrance to you and your people?" Eleanor added, "England is under attack."

The Prime Minister did not seem swayed in the least, "Mrs. Roosevelt, it would be an inspiration. Truly, I believe this would be most helpful to our cause."

The First Lady appeared to consider the idea for a few moments before stating finally, "Mr. Churchill, if you truly need my assistance, I would be happy to help." She paused and then added a query of her own, "I am wondering if I could ask for your help in a matter concerning Franklin's wellbeing?"

Winston leaned forward and said with complete sincerity, "Mrs. Roosevelt when it comes to assisting the President, you may ask me anything . . . anything at all."

After lunch, I took Horologium in hand and decided to move forward along the timeline to ascertain whether my Wayfarer influence had created the desired impact upon the ATL. I journeyed to later that very evening to the Rose Room where the Prime Minister was staying. After using the Horologium, within an instant my vaporous self stood next to the fireplace. Churchill had placed himself in a chair, where he took occasion to alternately smoke his cigar and then drink from a large goblet of brandy. The remnants of several cigars in the ashtray and the nearly empty bottle near his glass suggested that he had been engaged in such pastime for much of the evening. Although I had yet to encounter Churchill inebriated (in spite of his daily consumption), I felt the effects of alcohol within his mind and stood witness to his hand clumsily tapping cigar ashes into the ashtray before him.

As a means of discovering his resolve regarding Mrs. Roosevelt's visit to England, I extended my influence to feel his thoughts. At first, I became aware that the alcohol consumption had indeed exceeded his usual routine. I focused, and a moment later came to realize that he remained determined that such a trip by the First Lady would undoubtedly inspire and bolster his people. Additional thoughts came into my mind, and I could see that he and the President had already discussed Eleanor's visit for later in the new year. To be sure, I knew from my research within the library with George that this trip was destined to be the first of many, as Eleanor Roosevelt would travel the world for much of the war, so much so that the Secret Service would come to call her "Rover" for her continuous travels roving throughout the globe.

Confident that my mission had been a success, my ghostly hand took hold of the Horologium. I was about to press the "TEMPUS" button for the journey home when Winston Churchill glanced over his oval-rimmed glasses and stared directly at me in astonished surprise. "Mr. President?" he inquired in amazement.

My disbelief equaled his own, "You can see me?" I extended my influence to perceive what he was looking upon. A moment later, I understood that he could see but a faint outline of a human figure standing before him. The thought brought with it the awareness that although he could see a shadowy, ghostly presence, he could not hear me. All at once, the Prime Minister began to slowly rise from his chair, extending a quivering hand, "President Lincoln, I am most honored to meet you . . ." His palm reached out and passed through my ghostly self.

Believing it was truly my time to leave, I hurriedly took the watch in hand, pressed "TEMPUS" three times over, and immediately took my departure from the Roosevelt White House.

Although the encounter had provided me with a quick and unexpected jolt, on the journey home I reflected upon three thoughts that remained uppermost in my mind. The first was that my assignment with the First Lady had been a success. The second was the knowledge that what Emmett had never witnessed before was a target's ability to perceive the presence of a Time Traveler. And the third was the fact that Emmett had been nowhere to be found – making his awareness of my encounter with Churchill all the more worrisome to ponder.

Just as the Core chooses to empower one chain of events over another, humankind possesses its own capacity for personal decision and choice. The ATL is created in much the same manner as life unfolds — one choice, one decision, one direction at a time. For these reasons, the approved timeline is nothing more than the composition of countless choices that have been made in order to mold supremacy upon the very fabric of space and time.

For many, it may come as a surprise to learn that neither time nor any one life is ultimately dependent upon events that have occurred. We are not the result of those things that have happened to us. Neither is any timeline simply the consequence of historical events and incidents that have taken place. Instead, the ATL and even life itself are created through choices made by the League and the individual. Simply put, life is not created by what happens to an individual but instead by how that individual chooses to respond to what happens. Such is the enormity of personal co-creation.

Excerpt, "The Malleable Nature of Time," *Wayfarer's Manual — Continuing Education (revised edition);* **by Ruth #7**

THREE: *Journal Entry — December 16 ATL*

Although I have long been interested in things of a spiritual nature, heretofore I have chosen to maintain a healthy measure of skepticism regarding all subjects concerning same. For that reason, it was several days before I related the story of Lincoln's ghost seemingly wandering the corridors of the Roosevelt White House.

George and I sat at the small tabletop within our chambers. I had just finished describing my brief sightings of Ruth #7 during the mission and then proceeded to tell him what the First Lady had said about Mr. Lincoln's presence and the numerous individuals who had attested to the veracity of the matter. I finished my account, waiting for my roomie to respond.

He was somewhat amused as he stated, "And now, it seems, Prime Minister Winston Churchill would testify to the very same thing."

I responded, "That was me. I am speaking of those who truly encountered Lincoln for themselves."

"I understand," he replied, "but did you ever see or feel the former President?"

"No, but Eleanor and others were quite convinced of his presence." I paused for only a moment before inquiring, "George, do you believe in ghosts?"

"I am a Unitarian," he replied simply.

I shook my head in disagreement, "Having known several Unitarians, I can personally attest to the fact that they do not always agree on things of a spiritual nature." I restated my question, "What are your thoughts on an afterlife . . . or heaven?"

He smiled, "I believe a good Unitarian should be focused on making heaven here on earth." George then inquired, "What are your own thoughts on the afterlife? Your mind has explored all manner of subjects . . . what about this?"

"Well," I admitted, "I am a Deist—a Deist that frequently chooses to modify the parameters of just what that means."

"What does that mean in terms of an afterlife?"

I contemplated his query before responding, "Let me tell you a story." I leaned back in my chair and recollected a friendship of long ago, "When I was a young man, I had a friend named Charles . . . Charles Osborne. We shared many discussions, including those dealing with things of a spiritual nature. One afternoon, we swore an oath between us."

George's interest in the tale appeared heightened, as he leaned forward to listen.

I continued, "We promised each other that the first to die would revisit the other and reveal the various secrets of the afterlife . . . Not long thereafter, Charles died at a very early age." I stopped speaking and waited.

My roomie looked upon me for quite some period of time, and when it was clear he could stand the delay no longer, he asked with some semblance of force, "So tell me what happened?"

I leaned forward and whispered the words, "I have yet to hear from him."

Suddenly, we heard a knock at the door. Clearly frustrated with my tale, George rose to attend to the doorway. As soon as he turned the handle and began to open it, the scent of marvelous perfume rushed into our chambers. When the door was ajar, it revealed Louise #217 standing before us. Even in the doorway, the silkiness of her blonde hair and the intensity of her blue eyes were readily apparent.

Her French accent quickly acknowledged us, "Hello you two."

I rose from my chair and both George and I chimed in unison, "Hello, Louise."

Louise turned toward George and attempted a smile. "I hate to bother you," she said sweetly, "but I have been asked to bring you to the administrative offices."

I could not help but inquire, "What have you done now, George?"

George turned to me, looked back at Louise, and then once again turned in my direction.

"What have you done?" I questioned a second time. George fumbled for the words as he responded, "I may have made a few changes while I was visiting the Philippines . . ."

I interrupted, "Did these changes entail making ripples in history?" I could not help but smile.

"Well," George began with a sigh, "I decided to save several people from the virus that were not necessarily a part of my timeline assignment . . ."

Louise interrupted as she gently took hold of his arm, speaking softly, "Don't worry, George. The first violation of time travel protocols is only a written warning."

Neither myself nor my sometime roommate chose to mention the fact that this was not necessarily George's first violation.

After George had received his written warning and thereafter returned to our chambers, we decided to proceed to the League Café as it was mealtime and we longed for food as well as the camaraderie offered by our fellow Wayfarers. Since both Athena and Louise #217 were engaged in research within the Akasha library, George and I ventured to the repast on our own. When we neared the café doorway, I turned to George and inquired, "As we both know your history with time-rippling, were you by chance reminded of any ramifications should there be a second violation?"

"I was," he volunteered, repeating back the very words Sara #11 had spoken to him, "The second violation of time travel protocols will result in the confiscation of your Horologium, for a period to commiserate with the offense . . ."

"But not less than two weeks," I reminded him.

"And the third," George continued, "will result in a month-long probation from all League activities, including the League Café."

We entered the café, and I chuckled while patting him on the back, "Let us hope it does not come to that!"

"Or the fourth," George sighed, "and this horrible business of personal eradication."

"Most certainly."

We stood in line for only a moment, selecting our chosen fare. George opted for some manner of curry and potatoes, and I picked a helping of turkey and cranberries (with muffin and honey on the side), along with my coffee. Shortly thereafter, we found seats at the large table where the remaining graduates had seated themselves, along with Elder Professor Grimwald #94, who sat attentively listening to Manuela as she finished discussing her latest venture.

A member of the Core and an experienced educator, Grimwald possessed a kindly face the color of mahogany and a wealth of graying hair. He seemed to maintain an ongoing interest in the work we were all doing. He nodded approvingly as Manuela spoke.

She admitted, "I was most interested in this assignment even from the first."

"No doubt," Grimwald volunteered. He took a sip from his mug before continuing, "Cyrus certainly understood that providing his subjects with—what we would call—'human rights' would go a very long way in winning them over. When he released the Jews from Babylon and allowed them to return to Judah, he became the Emperor of Legend."

Manuela agreed, "Although the mission dealt with human rights, I saw how often Cyrus chose to ponder the outcome of his actions." She turned in my direction and smiled, "This assignment could have just as easily been undertaken by a diplomat."

"No doubt," Grimwald repeated, and then turned to look at George and me, "What activities have engaged the two of you of late?"

I smiled, "George and I have been making—what we are fond of calling—ripples in history."

George frowned but Grimwald responded immediately, "I like the sound of that!" He took another sip from his mug and seemed to cogitate the words for a moment or two before stating, "I believe we should add that to the curriculum. 'Ripples in history' . . . that certainly describes the work with which we are all involved, doesn't it?" He looked around the table for confirmation, prompting several of those present to nod their approval.

"So, tell me where have you been making these ripples?" the professor asked.

"I was in the Philippines, dealing with a coronavirus," George said only.

"And I was with Eleanor Roosevelt," I volunteered.

"I have long admired her," came Grimwald's reply. He took another drink from the mug and then looked around the table to make certain he had heard from everyone present. His eyes suddenly stopped their movement when they came to our Swede friend, "And what have you been doing, Emanuel?"

His response was quick, "I am attending to the reunification of the Church."

Grimwald's face appeared most surprised as he spoke, "I see . . . not an easy matter. Does the mission deal with the reunification of Anglicanism or Eastern Orthodoxy?"

"Eastern Orthodoxy," Emanuel replied, and then added, "I have yet to complete the assignment. Truly, it is a work in progress."

Bonne Soeur Marie replied encouragingly, "Recommencer . . . Begin again!"

"Yes," Grimwald agreed, "that is often the case in this work."

When Emanuel provided no further response, George volunteered, "Professor Grimwald, have you given any more thought to Emmett and his alternate timeline? I mean in terms of trying to eliminate some of the two thousand possibilities. That sounds like a lot."

Grimwald shook his head and disagreed, "To be exact, there are 2,857. I do not believe that any of them can be eliminated, George. I have already given the matter a great deal of thought. The logic to such a query is inescapable."

George was undeterred, "Remind us."

Elder Professor Grimwald leaned back in his chair and recounted the simple process he had used to arrive at such a number, "It really came from the realization that Emmett would require a timeline that had never been in opposition to our own. After all, his alternate timeline would need to become identical to ours if it had any chance of achieving complete supremacy." He glanced around the table to ascertain whether or not we understood the logic of such an assumption. "For that reason, Emmett needs a lesser timeline but nonetheless a very close replica."

After leaning forward to take a sip from his mug, he continued, "Since Emmett requires a timeline where there has never been an incident that sought supremacy against the ATL, it became obvious that no Time Traveler would have ever been dispatched on assignment to such a place. I then wondered if it would be possible to discern how many existing timelines within the Akasha had never been assigned a time-traveling mission. After a little help from the ATL Mission Office, we arrived at that very number. The answer is exactly 2,857. It is among one of those that Emmett's alternate will be found."

Manuela #64 interrupted, "Professor Grimwald, surely some of the timelines will not be a close replica to ours; they will just be lesser timelines."

The elder professor nodded in agreement, "Indeed, not all of them will be suitable as a possibility for Emmett."

"The number still sounds like a lot," George replied stubbornly.

"Perhaps," Grimwald agreed, "but it is certainly fewer than the infinite number we had considered previously."

A moment later, the professor rose from his seat, taking mug in hand, "I have a meeting to attend. Thank you all for this time together, it is much appreciated." He then turned in my direction, "Ben #239, remind me again what it is you and George call this business of time travel."

"We are making ripples in history," I replied.

Grimwald shook his head in the affirmative, "Ripples in history. I must tell the Core. We have got to get that terminology into the curriculum." He smiled at us and then took his departure from the café.

Much sooner than any of us desired, our personal schedules were soon interrupted by another of Agnes's "REQUIRED" continuing education classes. (I have emphasized "required" to better illustrate how our instructress is most fond of verbalizing this word.) We five sat obediently in the classroom as Agnes bounced about before us, seemingly collecting her thoughts for the instruction at hand. When she finally managed to compose herself, she leaned forward and spoke in a whisper as if imparting some tremendous secret.

"Today we will examine the Block Universe Theory," she said softly and then proceeded to bob about with enthusiasm. After such a display, she turned, writing the three words upon the board, and underlining each twice over for emphasis. As soon as the stylus underlines were complete, she looked back at the class and saw George waving his hand above his head. The interruption prompted a look of irritation on her face, but she inquired nonetheless, "Yes, George?"

"Miss Agnes," each time we have one of these classes, there are only five of us present for the required instruction . . ."

"And?" came her quick reply.

"I thought these continuing education seminars were mandatory for all Wayfarer graduates."

Her response was firm, "They are."

"Well, then where is everybody else?"

"And how many others are there?" I inquired for my own benefit. In spite of numerous attempts on my part, I had remained heretofore unsuccessful in discerning the true number of Time Travelers employed by the League.

Agnes scowled in my direction, "Ben #239, as you have been repeatedly reminded, that is a matter of Core business!" She turned back to George and said, "Obviously, the Akasha is recording everything that occurs within this classroom . . ." She looked once more in my direction and repeated, "Everything!" before concluding with, "Many of our Wayfarers take these classes at their convenience . . . after they have been recorded."

My sometimes roommate was quick to inquire, "Could we have the option to take them at our own convenience, as well?"

Her reply was immediate, "Absolutely not!"

George could not help himself, "Why do they have such an opportunity, while we do not?"

"Because you are here, and they are not!" Agnes shook her head in disgust, "Now where were we?"

Manuela #64 volunteered, "Senora, Agnes, you were telling us about the Block Universe Theory."

"Exactly!" Agnes slapped her desk for emphasis and looked out upon her charges. "Who remembers the ultimate truth about time?"

Our scholarly Swede was the first to respond, "Madame, Agnes, it is simply that the only moment is NOW."

She waved her stylus approvingly in his direction, "Correct!" and then leaned forward, "The Block Universe Theory has a similar premise. The theory is that everything that has ever happened, and everything that will ever happen, at any time, in any place, upon ANY timeline, is contained within the Block Universe."

While I attempted to cogitate upon what such a theory implied, our instructress nodded enthusiastically and continued, "Just imagine. It contains everything that has ever happened or ever will happen, at any time, in any place!" She lowered her voice again and whispered, "The past, the present, and the future are all equal and all real . . ."

It was Emanuel who interrupted, "It seems that such a theory is really no more than a partial understanding of the Akasha library." He was unimpressed, "Such a premise is not so extraordinary."

Agnes was not to be dissuaded. She shook her head in frustration and began waving the stylus in his direction. "Although there are similarities with the Akasha, let me assure you there are differences." She paused momentarily and then added, "The Block Universe contains everything that has ever happened and everything that ever will happen in any time . . ."

George interrupted, "Sounds like the Akasha library to me."

There was the sound of a bang as Agnes smacked the top of her desk a second time, "As I said, there are differences."

Soeur Marie was quick to inquire, "Comme quoi . . . like what?"

Our instructress took a deep breath and appeared to compose herself before replying, "The Block Universe contains four dimensions — there is length, height, width, and time." The statement appeared to give her some measure of personal satisfaction, as she nodded in the affirmative, "In the Block Universe, time does not pass, it just is."

She looked out upon the five of us as if to ascertain our grasp of such a concept before continuing, "The past, the present, and the future are no different from one another . . ."

"Sounds like the only moment is NOW," George replied.

Manuela agreed, "It sounds the same."

The next words that Agnes spoke were firm, "There are differences . . ."

Bonne Soeur Marie quickly raised her hand in the air, but Agnes ignored her.

"One of those differences," our instructress continued, "is that within the Block Universe time cannot be changed. According to the theory, if a time traveler were to go back in time, anything that time traveler did would simply make history exactly as it had always been . . ."

Emanuel raised his hand and then responded without waiting to be called upon, "This theory would appear to negate the very work with which we are all involved!"

Agnes was frustrated. She again pointed her stylus at him and appeared ready to speak when, suddenly, the Governor-General's voice came through the doorway, "Please excuse the interruption, Agnes."

I immediately turned to see Sara and ATL Mission Supervisor, Milton #71, standing before us.

Our instructress was quick to regain her composure, "Oh, Ms. Sara, it is so good to see you. What can we do for the two of you today?"

Sara turned to her companion and said only, "Milton, will you tell them?"

Milton appeared quite serious as he nodded, "Wayfarer graduates . . . friends. The Core has just met. It has been decided that effective immediately, we are restarting our efforts to find Emmett's alternate timeline. The matter continues to be the most serious issue we are facing. I have mission assignments for each of you." He raised his right hand to reveal multiple pieces of paper held within his grasp.

Agnes stood at the front of the room, bobbing about with renewed excitement, "Did you hear that? It's time for all hands on deck!"

Rather than taking time to describe the tedium of our "group orientation" that was called within the Akasha library immediately thereafter, it is perhaps only necessary to record the resulting outcome from such an assembly. Everyone within the League facility had been requested to come to the library's central meeting place.

As we gathered within the massive chamber and took our seats at one of the chairs that had been put in place, those members of the Core scheduled to speak to the assembly stood before us—Ruth #7, Milton #71, Elder Professor Grimwald #94, and the Governor-General, Sara #11.

In spite of the fact that several of us had already revisited his thought process, Grimwald spoke first, explaining to the gathering how he had arrived at the 2,857 timelines. Next came Sara, who took the opportunity to speak on two topics. First, she called to mind the eventual consequence of Emmett's alternate timeline. If successful, his work would undermine our own and take supremacy over the ATL. Once that occurred, he would be free to make any changes in world history he desired without consequence. She then reminded us that Emma #119 had been taken. (Although I could see many concerned faces within the assembly while she related the first item, I saw nary a look of concern when she detailed the second.)

After the Governor-General had finished her remarks, Ruth then provided us with a most helpful understanding of how those traveling to one of the designated timelines could quickly discern whether or not it was a likely possibility for Emmett's alternate. Her explanation was as follows, "Once given your assignment, you will need to pick an event in history with which you are most familiar. As Grimwald has told you, these possible timelines have never been in opposition to our own but that does not mean each of them will be an exact duplicate. Emmett needs a very close replica of the ATL. Your mission is to revisit a familiar period in history, and while you are there look around and see whether or not the timeline is unfolding the entire event just as you remember it . . ."

Manuela was quick to interrupt, "But Madame, remember your own words from the text, once we are there, the timeline will have altered ever so slightly."

"Correct," Ruth admitted, "but a visit is not enough to take it out of alignment with the ATL. Even if space-time is slightly different than your own experience on the ATL, those differences will be subtle, such as changes in clothing, and colors, and perhaps small variations in dialogue—the overall event and the outcome of such an event needs to be very closely aligned with your prior experience for it to be a possibility." She paused and presented us with a look of extreme seriousness, "If you believe you have found a possible alternate to the ATL, return to the League facility immediately. Do not try to confront Emmett on your own. We will need to assemble a large enough number to face him. Is that understood?" Several of those present nodded in the affirmative.

ATL Mission Supervisor, Milton #71 then proceeded to pass out what he called, "Your individual assigned timelines." It remained entirely unclear how these timelines were chosen, nor was there any elucidation as to why particular timelines were distributed to specific Wayfarers. From Milton's comments, I knew only that Elder Professor Grimwald read to the Core from his listing of possibilities, and that the ATL Mission Office signed off on those timelines that were ultimately selected.

After each traveler received an assignment, George turned to me and inquired, "Where are you going?"

"Timeline CMIV," I replied. "And you?"

He answered, "XXXVII," and then added, "I think I will look in on Carnegie."

I nodded, "I have several periods I am most drawn to, but I believe I should revisit Alexander . . . at least one more time."

After kissing my beloved Athena (and noting how Louise went out of her way to bid farewell to George, repeatedly reaching out to touch his arm as she spoke), I soon found myself traveling to timeline CMIV in order to revisit the banquet of one Alexander the Great—the very episode in the emperor's life that had brought the creation of Emmett's duplicate timeline to League's attention in the first place.

As I have often related the experience of falling as one takes part in these time-traveling ventures, there seems to be little reason for doing so again. However, I will note that during this particular descent, I quickly revisited my own calculations for the duration of time it was going to take us to explore each of the timelines appearing on Grimwald's list. I had originally assumed that in addition to five graduate Wayfarers and perhaps four or five members of the Core itself, the League might procure an additional seven or eight Time Travelers to deal with the problem. With that in mind and making certain that we continued to deal with (what Agnes is most fond of referring to as) "business as usual," I initially determined that collectively we could attend to perhaps 35 to 40 timelines per month. However, as this assignment was now the primary focus of the League's endeavors, I estimated we might undertake 50 or 60 timelines per month. Unfortunately, even at that pace, it would require somewhere around four years to visit each of the possible timelines. The result prompted me to remain sympathetic with George's overall assessment, "It sounds like a lot!"

Precisely as I had finished confirming my previous calculations, my descent came to an abrupt halt. I found my own consciousness within Alexander himself as he reclined at his banquet within the Babylonian palace. I became aware of the thoughts racing through his mind, which included a tremendous appreciation for the soldiers who surrounded him. As before, those most favored had taken positions near the emperor. These muscular warriors reclined (as did the emperor himself) upon couches and pillows, resting their heads upon one hand so that the other might reach for various foodstuffs that had been placed before them. Alexander did likewise. There was all manner of bread, and wine, and cheese, and fruit, and olives, and small pastry-filled morsels brimming with some semblance of meat or cheese. Young male attendants bustled about the room, refilling platters made of gold and silver, replenishing the wine, and receiving all manner of commands from those who had somehow been destined to a more desirable position in life than themselves.

As I witnessed the banquet repeat itself before me, I became aware that this emperor was much more balanced in temperament than any of the others I had previously encountered. To be sure, he possessed a wealth of military command and strategy. At the same time, however, I felt the talents of a diplomat, which frequently came to the forefront of his mind. He was also drawn to beauty — beauty in all its forms. This Alexander was loved and respected by those who followed him, but his overall disposition was more calming and reflective than the Alexander I had visited on the ATL.

As the emperor reached for another morsel to pass between his lips, I gave thought to separating myself, and in the next instant found I was standing next to him. Once again, the banquet and Alexander's most celebrated soldiers lay before me, and the smells of perfume, bread, cinnamon, foodstuffs, and men filled my nostrils. As I had already decided this could not be Emmett's alternate timeline, I took Horologium in hand for the journey home when suddenly, a deep, male voice came from behind, speaking my name aloud.

"Hello Ben," he said, and I swung about to see Emmett, former Keeper of the Records, and his dangling, white mane of hair standing before me.

"You are following me," I managed to reply.

"As I have told you. It is not that difficult to discover your whereabouts . . . or to know the activities of anyone within the League. How long do you think it was before I knew Bonne Soeur Marie had gone back to kill Phillip?" Emmett shrugged as though the matter was of little concern, "I could have addressed it immediately, but my attention has been elsewhere engaged."

I pondered the veracity of his words, "Could you tell me where Ruth is right now?"

He nodded, "I could." Emmett's hair brushed up against his robed shoulders as he spoke. "I have a number of ways of knowing what the League is doing."

"So, you have said."

Emmett restated the words he had asked previously, "Have you reconsidered my offer to join us?"

I shook my head and refused.

"You would find sufficient time for all that holds your interest."

I shook my head again.

"You could pursue your passions for science and invention . . . much has transpired since you had time to dabble in such pursuits."

When I gave no response, he continued, "You could explore any era or any head of state and have the time to examine all manner of politics, diplomacy, and business." He reminded me, "These are the activities that draw your interest. What about music and literature?"

I said nothing.

Finally, he added, "You could change the outcome of your relationship with Deborah . . . and the two of you could watch four-year-old, Franky, grow to become an adult. Absolutely nothing could stop you."

I ignored his words and inquired instead, "I have a question?"

He motioned toward me, "Proceed."

"What have you done with Emma #119?"

Emmett laughed outright, "I offer you everything you desire and instead you ask about Emma? I would imagine the League has found her departure a relief."

"What have you done with her?"

Emmett was unmoved, his deep voice added, "Do not worry yourself, she is fine . . . as fine as Emma can be."

I asked, "Why do you keep following me?"

"There are reasons," Emmett admitted, "for one, I miss our conversations. Surely, you feel the same?"

"I don't think so."

"Very well," Emmett sighed. His eyes opened wide, and he smiled, changing the subject at hand, "I assume you found the encounter with Churchill quite unusual."

"Most assuredly. Tell me how you knew such would occur."

He said only, "The Akasha."

I shook my head, "I don't think so."

Emmett replied, "Very well. We both know this is not the timeline you are seeking. I need to get back to my work." Suddenly, the old man smiled again and said, "Until we next meet, I wish you and George and the others every success as you continue to make these unnecessary 'ripples in history.'"

His words caused me to catch my breath, but before I could respond, he immediately vanished from my sight.

For whatever reason, those dealing with science have long maintained an assumption that their theories can never be proven, only substantiated. Obviously, this is confusing when considering the wealth of knowledge and insight possessed by the Core. Examples are numerous and include the many similarities between Moment One and the Big Bang. They comprise various connections between our own understanding of the Nature of Time (NOW) and scientific thoughts, theories, and premises regarding the same. They incorporate numerous studies that repeatedly verify how both motion and gravity impact time. The list continues.

What a Wayfarer should contemplate, however, is that these learned individuals have never encountered someone from any time period but their own. They have not had the opportunity to revisit even a solitary event from history. These scientists have never stood witness to perceiving the growth of consciousness laid out upon the fabric of space and time, and never once have they held a Horologium within the palm of their hand.

Excerpt, "Various Scientific 'Theories' Regarding the Feasibility of Time Travel," *Wayfarer's Manual— Continuing Education (revised edition);* **by Ruth #7**

FOUR: *Journal Entry—December 23 ATL*

After reviewing my latest journal entry, it became clear that I failed to chronicle the conversation with Ruth #7 that occurred following my fourth interaction with Emmett. As I have repeatedly discussed this encounter with both Athena and George (and the brief dialogue with Ruth that ensued thereafter), I mistakenly assumed that I had also recorded everything of note herein. In any event, Emmett had chosen the exact wording I had spoken to Professor Grimwald within the League Café but a short time earlier—"ripples in history." Obviously, this troubled me greatly. Although I had been cognizant of the fact that someone within the facility was relaying information to our former Keeper of the Records, it was hard to imagine that the elder professor himself could be that very individual. Perhaps Grimwald had instead repeated my expression to someone else and that person was responsible for passing the same words onto Emmett. Who did Grimwald tell? How many people did he tell? Was it possible that my thoughts about Grimwald #94 were entirely wrong? What if elder Professor Grimwald was not the Grimwald he claimed to be? Was it conceivable that he was working with Emmett? Worse yet, could the professor be one of those "duplicates" we often murmured about amongst ourselves?

These thoughts and others raced through my mind and I felt the need to talk to someone immediately upon my return. Clearly, I planned to discuss the matter at length with both Athena and George but—like myself —ultimately they could do very little to address the situation. It was for that reason that I sought out Ruth #7. Since I first became a part of the League, my experience with Ruth assured me that she could be trusted.

Since our facility is truly massive and I remained wary of telling anyone else that I sought her out, it took me the better part of an hour to discover Ruth's whereabouts. After walking through the hallway of the administrative offices, briefly exploring the café, and repeatedly knocking on the door of Ruth's personal chambers (where there was no response), I finally caught up with her as she was walking through one of the long passageways with Gregory #143. The two appeared to be returning from the Akasha library and were deep in conversation.

"I feel that I am of little use to you, or the League," Gregory spoke with complete honesty. Even within the hallway, his kindly face and his gentle spirit were readily apparent to me.

Ruth was adamant, "Nonsense! We need you now more than ever. I do not believe that Emmett has come to realize the potential danger of what he is doing." She shook her head in dismay.

Gregory responded, "The collapse of the ATL?"

Ruth stopped her pace and turned to us both. A look of grave concern fell upon her, "I am concerned about the collapse of the fabric of space-time itself."

I somehow managed, "I must beg forgiveness for the interruption but what do you mean the collapse of space and time?"

I was confused by the possibility, prompting Ruth to inquire, "Has Agnes covered the exclusion principle from physics?"

"The term is completely unknown to me,"

Ruth added, "It suggests that two identical objects cannot possibly occupy the same space at the same time. I am convinced that two identical timelines cannot coexist but would instead lead to the collapse of both or a paradox so extreme it is impossible to imagine."

We looked amongst ourselves for a moment until I managed to say again, "I beg forgiveness for interrupting the two of you, but I really need to speak with Ruth about a matter of grave importance."

Gregory looked in my direction and smiled, "It is not a problem." He turned to Ruth, "I will be in the café so that we might continue this discussion."

After he had proceeded down the hallway and turned the corner, I began, "We have not yet had a chance to converse since my experience at the Roosevelt White House. Did you discover anything further about the Emmett situation?"

She looked at me inquisitively but said nothing. After a moment of silence, I assumed she was still investigating the matter further. I then proceeded to describe my latest encounter instead, "I am returning from a conversation I just had with Emmett."

Her eyes sparkled with intensity, "What did you discuss?"

"Much of what we have discussed previously. He told me that he knew the whereabouts of everyone in the League, specifically mentioning you and me. He again invited me to join his work, offering everything he thought might be an enticement to me."

"The life of your son?"

I nodded, and then added, "I found myself very much alarmed by something he said moments before his departure . . . it was something I had just told Professor Grimwald only a few hours before when he was in the café with my classmates."

"What was it?"

I recalled, "He said, 'I wish you and George and the others every success as you continue to make these unnecessary ripples in history.'"

"He said what?" Ruth appeared more stunned than I had witnessed previously. She then admitted, "Grimwald used that exact term during our Core meeting. He informed us that was how you and George often refer to our work. He wanted to find a way to include it in the curriculum."

I nodded in agreement and soon inquired, "Are you thinking what I am thinking?"

"I'm afraid I am," she said somberly, "Unless one of the Wayfarers from your class is somehow involved, it would appear that Emmett is communicating with a member of the Core."

It was during our next scheduled continuing education class encounter that I immediately noticed how our instructress appeared more stressed than usual. After bobbing about in her typical fashion for several minutes, she leaned forward and took occasion to stare first at George, then at me, and shortly thereafter focused her attention on Emanuel. When she finally spoke, she made certain to focus her gaze back on each one of us in turn, "We have a lot to discuss this evening and we are going to get through this curriculum with as few interruptions as possible! Understood?"

The entire class fell silent, prompting Agnes to repeat her words more forcefully, "I said understood?"

Immediately, Bonne Soeur Marie and Manuela responded in unison, "Yes, Ma'am." Emanuel, George, and I looked between each of us before quickly replying in turn, "Absolutely," "Okay," and my own, "Understood."

Once that was out of the way, Agnes nodded to herself in complete satisfaction, took stylus in hand, and proceeded to describe the agenda, "Because you have all been recruited to find Emmett's timeline and still have personal missions awaiting you, and because you must attend to business as usual, we only have time for one seminar this week." She quickly glanced at George but before he could say a word, she added, "For that reason, we will need to cover two topics during tonight's seminar."

She turned to write on the board just as George lifted his arm in the air. As I was certain his query was meant to provoke her, I shook my head in disapproval. After giving it some consideration, he lowered his hand barely a moment before Agnes turned back to face us.

On the board, she had written (and underlined) two phrases: "Closed Timelike Curves" and "Carl Jung Time Slip," and proceeded to inform us, "These are our topics for this evening's discussion, and I want your complete attention!" She nodded again and began waving the stylus before us in her customary manner, "Now, who remembers what Einstein's Theory of Relativity suggests about time travel?"

Immediately, Emanuel and George each lifted a hand, followed close behind by Manuela. Agnes pointed the stylus at our Latin Wayfarer, "Yes, Manuela."

"Senora Agnes, relativity suggests that if you travel at the speed of light, time travel into the future is possible. It also suggests that time will move faster or slower depending upon the strength of gravity . . ."

Emanuel interjected, "The stronger the field of gravity, the slower time proceeds."

"Very good," Agnes acknowledged, "And what is one of the major problems with time travel suggested by relativity?"

"Causality!" George exclaimed before being called upon.

Our instructress pointed the stylus in his direction, "I need more details."

My sometimes roomie shrugged, "Very well. Time travel into the future is supported by relativity, but time travel into the past is more problematic . . ."

"In what way?" Agnes interrupted.

George continued, "If you go back and change the past it could unravel the same series of events that led to the very moment you came from. It creates a paradox."

"Exactly!" our instructress slammed the palm of her hand against the top of her desk, "And that is where the concept of Black Holes, Wormholes, and Closed Timelike Curves come in. These are the scientific premises that make theories of time travel possible."

After taking time to write and underline these words on the board, Agnes appeared to be quite pleased with herself. For the hour that ensued, she proceeded to provide additional details on the various topics of mention, only a portion of which came to me with any semblance of clarity and understanding. She proceeded to draw several forms that were somewhat similar to an hourglass and described how the top portion of these forms suggested the capacity of traveling forward in time within said "Closed Timelike Curve," whereas the lower portion was tantamount to a journey backward in time. Her oration continued for quite some time, prompting me to surmise that her primary focus was not on whether her listeners had any comprehension of the subjects being presented, only that the subjects were being discussed. In spite of being confused throughout much of her presentation, I managed to take away several concepts from that portion of the evening's curriculum.

Firstly, although their existence has never been proven, for some reason, there appears to be a great deal of scientific conjecture on the topic of wormholes — tunnels through the fabric of space-time that are thought to somehow connect two separate moments in time.

Secondly, there is little agreement among scientists about the nature of these Closed Timelike Curves. Are they even possible? If so, would they allow for time travel only to the future? Might they instead permit time travel to the past, but only as far as the time traveler's initial point of departure?

And finally, I found myself possessing a great deal of gratitude that these required continuing education programs were no longer subject to the tests and exams that had long been a component of our previous undergraduate studies.

After Bonne Soeur Marie had asked for clarification on a couple of matters, Agnes turned to erase everything from the board except for the underlined "Carl Jung Time Slip." When only these words remained before us, she spun herself around, pointed her stylus at the phrase, and informed us, "We are going to discuss the Carl Jung Time Slip. Now let me make several things quite clear . . ."

George quickly turned to me and silently mouthed the words "Background information."

She stared directly at my roomie, "For everyone's information, he was a Swiss psychiatrist and had once been a colleague of Sigmund Freud's. He would come to be known as the founder of analytical psychology." She turned to write that phrase upon the board and proceeded to inform us, "Jung never referred to this as a time slip. In fact, it is entirely unclear whether or not he was even familiar with the term. Jung believed that what he witnessed and what I am about to describe was simply a projection of his anima . . ."

At the mention of such a word (which was completely unknown to me), Bonne Soeur Marie's hand shot up into the air, prompting our instructress to say, "Jung considered the anima to be the feminine part of an individual's personality . . ."

Emanuel interrupted, "The word remains unclear to me."

Soeur Marie's hand continued waving in the air and Manuela's followed close behind. Agnes shook her head in frustration, waved the ever-present stylus before her, and said, "Let me finish some background information and then . . . and ONLY then, I will be happy to answer any questions you might have!"

She sighed and asked rhetorically, "Where was I? Oh yes . . . As I was saying, Carl Jung never referred to this as a time slip. When he told the story in his biography, *Memories, Dreams, Reflections,* he described the experience as 'fascinating.' Years later, some of his colleagues would agree that his experience had been a projection of the anima, others would . . ."

George raised his hand, causing Agnes to shake her head, while saying, "Let me continue!" She added, "Others would try to disprove what he had seen with his own two eyes, saying that they believed he had simply misremembered the event." She smiled approvingly, "But you know what? He had a witness with him who saw the very same thing. This is the Carl Jung Time Slip."

Agnes leaned forward and spoke as though revealing some amazing secret, "This took place in the city of Ravenna, in northeast Italy, right after Jung had visited the tomb of Galla Placida . . ."

Once again, Bonne Soeur Marie #304 lifted her hand into the air, but our teacher chose to ignore her, instead continuing, ". . . Galla Placida was an early follower of Christianity. She was the daughter of the Roman emperor Theodosius, and until her death in 450 AD, she would have a major role in Roman politics for decades. It was her tomb that Carl Jung and his companion, Toni Wolff, visited in 1932."

Upon completion of the background information, our instructress appeared to sigh with some measure of relief. She proceeded to bounce about for a moment or two before the tale recommenced, "The two ventured into the Baptistery of Neon, which is the most ancient monument in the city—a major tourist attraction. All at once, they became aware of a beautiful blue light that filled the room." Agnes leaned forward and stated mysteriously, "But neither Jung nor his companion could find a source for that light."

She resumed, "Next, they were startled by the beauty and magnificence of four mosaic frescoes upon each of the enormous walls within the baptistery. Each presented a colorful scene from the scriptures. Two drew their attention more than the others—one showed the children of Israel crossing the Red Sea; another portrayed Peter attempting to walk upon the Sea of Galilee but stumbling because of his lack of faith. Each of the mosaics was in pristine condition."

Our teacher forcefully slapped the top of her desk— prompting George and I to jump in our seats. She said only, "Keep in mind, these were exquisite frescoes! Jung and Ms. Wolff spent as much time as they could admiring each of the scenes until their schedule demanded that they needed to depart. They left the baptistery, the blue light, and the four incredible mosaics behind, and hurried toward the vendor stalls where Jung hoped to find postcards of the frescoes they had just admired before they departed."

Agnes shook her head in the negative, "Although the two found hundreds of postcards, not one depicted the colorful scenes they had visited. Jung expressed his disappointment and reassured Ms. Toni that he would try to order the postcards upon returning to Zurich. The two went back to Switzerland.

A few weeks later, Jung was overjoyed when a friend stated his own plans to travel to Ravenna. Jung excitedly told the friend about the Baptistery of Neon, the four amazing frescoes, and his personal desire for pictures, postcards, or both."

Our instructress stopped speaking and glanced at each of us, nodding with satisfaction. We waited for further comment but there was none. Finally, Soeur Marie could wait no longer and asked impatiently, "Ce qui c'est passé? What happened?"

Agnes smiled, "The friend went to Ravenna and returned a few weeks later. Upon his return, he came to see Jung and Ms. Wolff and explained that he had been unable to obtain either the postcards or the photographs, because the mosaics did not exist. Jung and Ms. Wolff appeared very much confused by his claim, but he repeated the statement several times over, 'They do not exist!' According to the story, Ms. Wolff spoke with certainty, 'I saw them with my own eyes!' but the friend insisted that there were no frescoes to be found."

Agnes leaned forward, "As it turned out, the frescoes were not there, because they had been destroyed hundreds of years earlier. They had once been within the walls of the baptistery, but they were gone." The slightest of smiles began to appear on her face. "Now what is truly amazing is that these frescoes existed during the lifetime of Galla Placida but no more. It was for that reason that Jung beleived that a portion of his and Ms. Wolff's unconscious minds had somehow merged with the unconscious mind of the deceased Galla Placida, and the two had seen the baptistery and the frescoes just as the emperor's daughter had once seen them. Carl Jung called the experience one of the most curious events in his entire life!"

She nodded one last time before concluding, "Now, you and I know this had nothing to do with the unconscious mind . . . what foolishness! Obviously, this was a time slip — the Carl Jung Time Slip."

As my frequent encounters with Alexander had become somewhat monotonous to ongoing personal exploration, I decided instead to revisit Edward VIII, King of the United Kingdom, and Emperor of India for our continuing "all hands on deck" assignment. After all, the purpose of these missions was simply to find any timeline event that appeared identical to an experience we had previously witnessed upon the ATL, thereby making it a possible contender for Emmett's alternate. With that premise squarely in mind, once again each of us was presented with a possible location for the alternate timeline by the ATL Mission Office. After embracing my beloved Athena and bidding a fond farewell (with promises of a romantic encounter upon my return), I ventured forth to further explore the matter on my latest assignment — timeline MII.

My previous forays into the Akasha library and my own prior experience with Edward (called "David" by his family and those to whom he was closest) had familiarized me with the proper unfoldment of history according to the ATL. For whatever reason, Edward was repeatedly drawn to liaisons with married and divorced women who were prone to exerting some manner of maternal influence upon him. This behavior was common knowledge to many and somewhat appalling to some. Certain members of the British aristocracy had even come to question Edward's suitability as heir to the throne. I also learned from the Akasha that while the prince traveled by train with married English socialite Freda Ward (apparently enthralled with the company of each other), Winston Churchill had once observed them together and commented, "It is quite pathetic to see the Prince and Freda. His love is so obvious and undisguisable . . ."

Not long thereafter, the prince's scandalous behavior rose to an even greater level of concern when Freda was supplanted by none other than an American! She was the divorced and remarried Viscountess Thelma Furness, whose own mother had provided her (and her twin sister, Gloria) with stern relationship advice to "marry rich and marry well." Both girls had done just that. Gloria had married a Vanderbilt and Thelma had found herself a Viscount — only one level below a duke! Neither girl found happiness, however, as Gloria soon sought a divorce and Thelma's second husband, Marmaduke, frequently pined after his deceased first wife, finding some semblance of relief only in alcohol and his work. The situation prompted Thelma to look elsewhere for companionship, which she soon found in the company of the Prince of Wales. They were together for years until Thelma introduced the prince to yet another divorced and remarried American, Wallis Simpson. Ironically, the two women had much in common, although Wallis was much thinner and demanding and Thelma seemed to possess an enduring fondness for both hats and pearls. In the end, however, it was Wallis that the ATL held responsible for a king's abdication of the British throne.

After only a moment of reacquainting myself with things as they should be concerning the Prince of Wales, I turned the hands of my Horologium to the left, gave thought to a conversation I had once witnessed between the prince and his father, and repeated an incredibly long name, "Edward Albert Christian George Andrew Patrick David Windsor." Afterward, I pressed the "TEMPUS" button, took a deep breath, and began to fall.

I have found that traversing such a short distance into the past is relatively brief in duration when compared to the prolonged interval one must navigate when traveling to ancient times in pursuit of one such as Alexander. For this reason, it was not long thereafter when I found myself within the personage of the Prince of Wales, sitting across the desk from his father, King George V.

"It is inappropriate," the king coughed several times, yet stubbornly persisted to smoke his cigarette, ". . . inappropriate that my son and heir to the throne should continue in these illicit liaisons with married and divorced women. This must stop!" As soon as the words were spoken, he coughed anew.

I felt the frustration and anger pass through Edward's mind as he stared with contempt at his father. Of late, the king was becoming an ever-greater nuisance in the prince's life. To be sure, Edward wanted to be left alone.

King George inhaled from his cigarette, coughed again, and continued, "The time has come for you to settle down. You must find a wife who is fit to become queen . . . Do you understand? It is your duty to the Empire!"

Edward responded angrily, "I did not choose to be King!"

The King's words grew louder, "Nor did I, but it is the burden and duty that has been thrust upon us!"

The prince was unmoved, "No one can tell me what to do, Father."

The king nodded, "And that has always been your greatest problem." George shook his head in dismay and placed the remnants of his cigarette in the ashtray before him. Edward continued to stare in anger.

King George moved to speak but stopped, as if reconsidering his thoughts. Suddenly, he chose a different approach, "Your brother, Albert . . . Bertie found Mary. I have no doubt that you can find someone equally suitable if you only try."

Edward was unmoved, "I can only be myself." The prince shook his head in disgust and rose from the chair.

"We have not finished!" the king was aggravated.

"I need to go."

Breaking all manner of protocol, Edward walked quickly toward the room's doorway, opened the door, and briefly acknowledged the presence of someone standing in the hallway. He turned to inform his father, "The Prime Minister wishes to see you." A moment later, he was gone.

The king spoke, rising from his chair, "My dear Baldwin, please come in." He motioned for Stanley Baldwin, the Prime Minister, to take the seat before him.

After sitting, Baldwin managed to inquire, "How was the conversation, Your Majesty?"

"Not good . . . not good at all." The king opened his desk drawer, fumbled with a package of cigarettes, and took one in hand. A moment later it was lit, prompting him to take a long draw, followed by a cough, and then the words, "After I am dead, I fear that boy will ruin himself within a year." He coughed before adding, "I fear he is not fit for the throne."

Baldwin sighed before managing the words, "I regrettably agree, Your Majesty. We must find a way to do what is best for the country."

The king nodded, "For the empire."

Although what I had witnessed bore some resemblance to the same situation upon the ATL, it was far from a duplicate. Nonetheless, I surmised that Emmett might be able to mold such a timeline into one suitable for his purposes. For that reason, I took

Horologium in hand and chose to explore the moment of Edward's abdication.

To be sure, such a distance in time travel was quite brief, so the actual trip took on the nature of a leap more than any semblance of a fall but, nonetheless, I soon found myself sitting at His Imperial Majesty's desk, with several typed pages grasped before me, facing an enormous microphone. My own ghostly hands appeared to swirl in vaporous forms of motion around and through the hands of the king—King Edward VIII. I could feel his apprehension as he sat looking at the director of the BBC who spoke a few words of introduction.

"This is Windsor Castle, His Royal Highness . . ." The director pointed in his direction, giving him the signal to begin the global broadcast.

He began, nervously at first, "At . . . At long last, I am able to say a few words. I have never wanted to withhold anything, but until now it has not been constitutionally possible for me to speak . . ."

As he continued, his voice became stronger, "A few hours ago I discharged my last duty as King and Emperor, and now that I have been succeeded by my brother, the Duke of York, my first words must be to declare my allegiance to him. This I do with all my heart . . ."

I found myself listening as bystander until the memorable words were spoken, "I have found it impossible to carry the heavy burden of responsibility and to discharge my duties as king as I would wish to do without the help and support of the woman I love . . ."

I could not help but confirm the close similarities between the abdication on timeline MII and the one upon the ATL. Suddenly, however, Edward moved his eyes from the papers before him to the other side of the room where he gazed in infatuation at his intended. I turned and found myself somewhat surprised to see a woman wearing an enormous strand of pearls — Viscountess Thelma Furness.

As such, it became immediately apparent that this was not Emmett's timeline. I took hold of my Horologium and departed from England.

Obviously, maintaining the ongoing growth of human consciousness has long been the central purpose of the League. It underlies the entire formation of the ATL, and it motivates the vast majority of the Core's involvement in all manner of timeline adjustments. Personal consciousness realigning itself with countless moments in history across innumerable timelines has become a way of life for every Wayfarer. Besides its exploration of timelines and the Akasha, the Core has come to understand that even a mind's solitary exploration of the past is nothing less than a rudimentary form of human consciousness undertaking the experience of time travel.

In consideration of all of these things, clearly, consciousness is fundamental to the human condition. It is also essential to the perception of time. What may come as a surprise, however, is that one's individual consciousness cannot be shared with another. It is simply personal consciousness. For that same reason, it should be made clear that time will forever remain a specific reality only to the individual perceiving it.

Excerpt, "Time Travel and the Components of Consciousness," *Wayfarer's Manual — Continuing Education* **(revised edition); by Ruth #7**

FIVE: *Journal Entry — January 2 ATL*

In spite of my ongoing commitment to Athena and repeated attempts to push any thoughts to the contrary far from my mind, I must confess that I still find myself hopelessly drawn to beautiful women. Having experienced this attraction ever since the days of my youth and finding myself subject to this same inclination up to the time of my personal recruitment, I have come to believe that such might simply be the fate of a predominant portion of the male sex. (I note herein that even the ancient gods themselves were not immune to the power of Cupid's arrow.) To be sure, whenever I am in Athena's presence, I do not find myself prone to this malady to the same extent. However, when she is not around, I cannot assuage the fear that I might too easily succumb to my lifelong affliction.

In any event, perhaps out of a desire for self-preservation, I became convinced that I needed to use whatever influence I possessed to make certain it would be my roomie George who found himself within Louise's bedchamber rather than myself. The opportunity to exert some encouragement in that very direction presented itself when my fellow classmates gathered in the café to discuss their most recent "all-hands-on-deck" timeline missions. Each of my co-Wayfarers provided some semblance of rationale for why they had chosen their specific targets within the ATL Mission Office assigned timeline. Our studious Swede volunteered to go first.

Emanuel sat across the table from George and me. We had placed ourselves at — what the café staff is fond of calling — an "eight-top" in spite of the fact that there were but five of us present. There was an open seat next to Emanuel, one available next to me, and an empty space at one end of the table. Our collective hope was that both Athena and Louise would finish their labors shortly and join us for the company and fellowship provided by such occasions.

Emanuel began, "My assignment was timeline MDLXXIII. Having had an extremely positive experience during my previous mission with the Pharaoh Akhenaten, I decided to choose him once again as my target." He looked around the table, seemingly observing only a faint recognition of the name, which prompted him to provide some additional background information.

"Surely, some of you remember Akhenaten?" He continued, "He was the pharaoh who broke from the old Egyptian religion and promoted the idea of monotheism, one God — Aten. He moved the capital city to Armana." When there came no response, he added, "He was the husband of Nefertiti and the father of Tutankhamun."

At the mention of such names, several heads nodded within our group while George replied, "Certainly, I remember."

"Good," our Swede answered in relief. "My mission proved to be only a lesser timeline. Things were not at all identical to the ATL. This Akhenaten was poisoned by the Egyptian priests as soon as he attempted to displace the longstanding Egyptian gods with his own."

George response was mocking, "Great, that means we only have to examine 2,856 more."

"Make that 2,855," I answered immediately. "I also found my assignment upon timeline MII was no threat to the ATL. I decided to return to Edward VIII, and although he possessed many of the same characteristics as his counterpart on the approved timeline, his choices were not all in keeping with the sanctioned course of history."

The five of us looked about the table for the next volunteer until Manuela #64 moved to speak, "My mission sent me to examine timeline CCXXII. Because I had been so impressed by their efforts during my first encounter, I chose to revisit Senores Hine and Murphy . . ."

"The advocates of child labor laws," Emanuel interrupted, proving yet again that he was often the most attentive among us.

"Exactly!" Manuela concurred, and then reminded those present, "Remember, Edgar Gardner Murphy was a minister who spoke out against child labor, and Lewis Hine was a photographer who captured images of children working under quite dangerous conditions?"

There appeared quick recognition of their efforts around the table.

Our Latin classmate continued, "Just as was the case with the ATL, Edgar used his writing talents to bring this horrible abuse of children to the public's attention. Because of his efforts and Hine's pictures, the National Child Labor Committee was created in New York and laws throughout the country soon brought an end to much of the child labor that had existed . . ."

I found myself interrupting, "Was the timeline a possible alternate for Emmett's purposes?"

"It was," Manuela conceded, "I need to report it to the ATL Mission Office."

A female voice and the rich scent of French perfume both came to my senses at the very same moment, "What do you need to report to the office?" she asked.

I spun around in my seat to see Louise #217 and Athena standing behind me. I quickly patted the chair beside me, smiled at Athena, and assured her, "I have been saving this for you."

Louise smiled in my direction but proceeded around the table to take the seat next to Emanuel (and across from George). She repeated herself, "What do you need to report to the office?"

Manuela nodded, "I found a possible location for Emmett. Timeline CCXXII could be an alternate. They need to add that timeline to the possibility list."

George sighed, "That leaves us with only 2,854 more to examine."

My Mediterranean sweetheart looked to George on my other side and responded, "Still trying to eliminate timelines, George?"

George shrugged, "It's going to take us forever."

Manuela interjected, "George, in all likelihood the alternate will be found before we explore every one of those timelines. You also need to remember that other Wayfarers and members of the Core are searching as well . . . We won't be responsible for all of them."

"It is still going to take a very long time!" George insisted.

Louise reached across the table, gently patting his hand as she spoke, "Mon chéri, do not worry yourself," she said sweetly. "You are making great progress." She turned to Manuela acknowledging, "I will tell Milton about this timeline."

As she spoke, I could not help but notice how the overhead lights highlighted her glistening skin and the silkiness of her blonde hair. Her blue eyes soon turned back in Athena's and my direction, prompting me to divert my gaze.

She asked, "Did anyone else find another possible alternate?" She seemed to be speaking directly at me.

In spite of the fact that the strong scent of perfume continued to envelop my nostrils, I turned and pointed at Manuela instead, managing to respond, "Only Manuela so far. Both Emanuel and I found timelines not exactly in accord with the ATL."

For my own safety, I quickly looked to Athena. She appeared to be taking it all in before inquiring, "What about Bonne Soeur Marie and George?"

"Mon tour . . . my turn," Soeur Marie declared, and then turned to George, "If this is okay with you?"

George appeared indifferent, motioning her to proceed, "Go ahead."

"Very well." She began, "My assignment was timeline LXXXIV. I chose to once again visit the mama of the President, Nancy Hanks."

As she spoke, George turned inquisitively to me; I said only, "Abraham Lincoln."

Bonne Soeur Marie continued, "Remember, this was my mission with Milk Sickness? The poor woman lost her life to this illness on the ATL. Her fate was much the same on my timeline mission. Although it was similar, it was not the same . . . a lesser timeline to be sure."

"We're at 2,853," George volunteered.

I turned back to my roomie, "You're next. Make it 2,852."

George nodded.

Louise smiled, and pleaded with him, "Oh, yes. George, I would love to hear about your experience."

George seemed somewhat hesitant with the attention, but he responded nonetheless, "I chose as my target Carnegie — Andrew Carnegie . . ."

I interrupted, "Wasn't he a businessman and philanthropist, much like yourself, George?"

George appeared confused but replied nonetheless, "He was."

I added, "Didn't you tell me about his passion for libraries . . . much like your own?"

His look of confusion grew, "He did. Why do you ask?"

I feigned innocence. "No reason," I replied. "I just recall so many of the things you told me about this Carnegie fellow. I think it's fascinating that the two of you have so much in common."

"I see," was his response, he then proceeded, "My assignment was with timeline CCCXXV. I chose Carnegie because of his passion for philanthropy."

I interrupted again, "As I recall, you told me his wife's name was Louise."

I looked directly across the table at Louise, "I believe he married a woman named Louise."

George sounded cautious, "He did."

Louise reached out, taking George's hand from the tabletop. "That is just amazing, George," she smiled sweetly, "Tell me more."

My roomie cautiously withdrew his hand from hers and continued, "In any case, Carnegie believed in giving away his wealth during his lifetime."

"That's exactly what you did, George." I added, "Isn't it?"

George appeared all the more perplexed but managed to say, "There were several major differences in the timeline. For example, there was no Harwich Mine disaster . . ."

Before he could say another word, Bonne Soeur Marie lifted her hand in the air, prompting him to add, "The disaster killed almost 200 people, including a 15-year-old boy. According to the Akasha, it was one of the motivations that prompted Carnegie's interest in philanthropy. He even matched the government's relief moneys with his own personal contribution."

I inquired, "Didn't you tell me that he set up a major foundation to distribute contributions for public projects even after his death?" Before awaiting a reply, I added, "I believe you said his wife, Louise, gave up her right to his estate so that his wealth could be used just as he intended." I looked directly at Louise, who quickly winked at me in understanding.

Louise #217's interest in the tale was suddenly heightened, "I would love to hear more about this other Louise. What was her name before she wedded her philanthropist?" (I should note that Louise emphasized the word "wedded.")

George managed to stammer, "Louise Whitfield."

"George, why don't you take our Louise to the Akasha and show her some of what you told me?"

A look of fear crossed his face. At the same moment, Louise reached out and touched his hand, "Oh, yes, George, I would love to see all that you know!"

Immediately, Louise rose from the table and came around to take him by the arm. He looked nervously around the table for someone to come to his rescue, but no one made a move. She continued to tell him how fascinated she was by the story and how she wanted to hear much more about "this amazing philanthropist." A moment later, she had managed to drag him from the café.

Athena turned to me, "What are you trying to do?" she inquired.

"Helping a friend overcome his shyness," I replied.

Athena frowned, "I hope you know what you're doing."

Only Bonne Soeur Marie voiced a response, "Moi aussi . . . me too."

We looked quietly amongst ourselves and said no more until Athena chose to ask several questions about Emanuel's and Manuela's latest mission assignments. Afterward, we exchanged pleasantries and made plans to regroup for suppertime. Just as my classmates began to depart, I attempted to rise but Athena quickly pulled me back in my chair.

"I need to talk to you," she said softly.

For that reason, we remained in place, bidding farewell to the others and waiting until they were all gone. When we were alone, my sweetheart turned to me and spoke what had been on her mind.

"From what I heard, each of you is reporting to the ATL Mission Office when you find a possible alternate for Emmett's timeline?"

I said only, "We are."

"And is anyone from the ATL Mission Office or the Core itself telling you when they find a possible alternate?"

I was confused, "I don't understand."

Athena looked directly into my eyes, "Aren't members of the Core taking part in these assignments?"

"Yes, they are. I already told you I saw Ruth in the Roosevelt White House, looking further into this issue with Emmett."

My sweetheart appeared to frown, "Isn't the ATL Mission Office and the Core deciding which timelines get assigned to each Wayfarer?"

"They are." I remained uncertain as to what she was trying to say.

"Didn't you tell me that you feared someone on the Core was communicating with Emmett?"

I paused momentarily before responding, "I did."

"Ben, if someone on the Core knows where Emmett is, they're never going to assign that timeline to one of you . . . they will make certain it is assigned to them. If a member of the Core is really involved, they're not going to divulge Emmett's location."

I gasped, "You're right!"

Athena nodded, "They will make sure that no one knows. I think this 'all-hands-on-deck' assignment is nothing more than a diversion."

"You don't think Ruth is involved, do you?" I asked quickly.

Athena shook her head, "I don't know what to think."

Our collective group supper that evening took place without either of us divulging Athena's latest thoughts regarding Emmett and our ongoing search for timelines. It had also occurred without the presence of either George or Louise. They were not in attendance when such plans were discussed, but it was rare for my roomie to miss out on any nourishment provided by the café unless, of course, he was somewhere involved on a timeline mission. Rather than a timeline assignment, however, I hoped that he was elsewhere engaged in the company of Louise.

Our get-together was pleasant enough, and after our food had been consumed and the gathering had reached its conclusion (with still no sight of either George or Louise), I bid farewell to my sweetheart and journeyed to the classroom, where I took my seat for yet another of Agnes's regularly scheduled continuing education seminars. For a few moments, I could not help but contemplate whether or not George had finally succumbed to the allures of silken skin and French perfume. The images that danced briefly through my mind, however, were quickly discarded when he hurried into the classroom and nearly threw himself into his seat beside me. He said nothing, choosing instead to stare straight ahead. Our instructress had yet to arrive.

Although George was silent, I could not help but inquire, "How did it go with Louise?"

"Don't ask!"

He appeared angry, so I attempted a more supportive approach, "Do you want to talk about it later?"

He turned and glared at me, "I hold you partially responsible!"

I was about to query further as to the exact nature of what I was partially responsible for when Agnes bobbed through the doorway. She was followed close behind by her Middle Eastern companion "from the old days" — Nashwa #86. I was near to surmising that Nashwa was to be our guest speaker when Agnes took the stylus from atop her desk and waved it in our direction.

She sighed with adoration, "We are so lucky to have Nashwa with us this evening! She has a very special announcement." She turned to the other woman, smiled, and extended her arm to pass the stylus, but Nashwa simply shook her head, "No."

"I don't think I'll need that, Agnes," Nashwa replied.

Our instructress was surprised, "Are you sure? You might want to write something down!"

"I'll be fine," Nashwa assured her.

Agnes appeared disappointed but nonetheless took a seat near the front of the room. Nashwa smiled at us and proceeded to share her announcement.

"I think I may have told you previously that I have had some very interesting experiences as a Wayfarer . . ."

Agnes interrupted from her seat, "She's had an amazing career!"

Nashwa ignored the outburst and continued, "As you probably know, I've been asked to take on the Core's responsibilities for new student recruitment. I want to do things a little differently than my predecessor."

"Emma," George whispered just under his breath.

Bonne Soeur Marie lifted her hand high into the air and inquired, "Madame, will we be required to leave our personal quarters?"

"Pardon me?" Nashwa appeared confused.

Soeur Marie sounded worried, "Nouveaux étudiants . . . new students! When they arrive, will they take our rooms?"

"Absolutely not," the woman was quick to respond. "We have plenty of rooms. Besides, there will be a number of personal investigations before any new recruit is chosen. Those who do arrive will be given rooms but you'll be free to decide to stay here and continue working from headquarters. You might instead pursue a career in the field. The choice is entirely yours to make."

I asked what had immediately come to mind, "What kind of personal investigations?"

"That's a matter of Core business!" Agnes announced from her seat, shaking her head in disgust.

Nashwa relented, "It's okay, Agnes. I don't think it is a state secret or anything." She nodded her head and volunteered, "Much of it is research in the Akasha. We also like to have a conversation with each candidate before they are actually chosen as a student."

It was George who responded, "What? You actually interviewed each of us before we became students?"

"It wasn't me," she was quick to respond, "but either Emma or another member of the Core would have had a conversation with each of you before you made the list of finalists . . ."

Emanuel interrupted, "I don't remember such a conversation." He appeared most certain.

Manuela added, "Neither do I."

Nashwa smiled, "This would have happened long before your personal recruitment. Most likely, it would have gone unnoticed among your life's events."

Agnes had had enough, "Nashwa is here to give an announcement, not debate the recruitment process. That is a matter of Core business!"

"It's okay," Nashwa reassured us. "I am just here to say that I would love to have your new student recommendations. Just get them to my office."

Bonne Soeur Marie's hand shot up into the air a second time, "Someone we know?"

"It can be someone you know personally, someone you know from history, or even someone you've encountered on a travel assignment. Anyway, that's all. I would love to have any recommendations you think are appropriate in the next couple of weeks."

Nashwa thanked the class, turned us back over to Agnes, and took her departure from the room.

Agnes walked to her place at the front of the classroom, shook her head in dismay, and sighed. When she appeared to gather her composure, she took stylus at the ready, and began.

"As you know, there are those within the scientific community who have long maintained an interest in the possibility of time travel." She lowered her voice to speak in a whisper, "Of course, quite a number prefer to keep their interest a secret to avoid ridicule from their peers." She nodded, apparently agreeing with her statement, waved the stylus before us, and exclaimed with more enthusiasm than seemed necessary for an evening seminar, "Tonight, we are going to explore three major scientific theories about time travel!"

"Oh, joy," George uttered aloud.

His outburst prompted me to assume that he had at least recovered somewhat from his encounter with Louise.

"What?" Agnes turned in his direction and glared.

My roomie responded quickly, "I'm just very excited about this discussion."

Our instructress frowned for only a moment before turning to write three phrases upon the board: "Fixed Timeline," "Dynamic Timeline," "Multiverse Timeline." Once they had been appropriately underlined, she took a step back, stared at the whiteboard before her, and nodded approvingly, "Let us begin with the theory of time travel within the concept of a fixed timeline."

She looked about the classroom and appeared deep in thought. After taking some time to gather her thoughts, she resumed her discussion, "I want to explain these theories as simply as possible. The challenge is that it is hard to completely separate some of these ideas, as there is overlap, but I am going to try and make them as understandable as possible."

With that, she turned back to the board and used the stylus to draw a straight line before us, traversing from the left side of the board to the right. When the line was in place, just above the middle of the line, she drew a stick figure. The figure appeared to be some representation of a person.

"If you are a Time Traveler," she pointed toward the stick figure, "in some theories of a fixed timeline, you can only travel into your own future." She drew an arrow from the stick figure pointing to the right side of the board. "However, there are others who subscribe to the fixed timeline theory who contend that time travel into the past is possible with one major limitation."

Agnes proceeded to draw a corresponding arrow pointing to the left side of the board and informed us, "These individuals believe that any changes you think you are making to the past were already a part of history to begin with. In other words, anything that happens was meant to happen. A Time Traveler cannot change the past on a fixed timeline." She looked out at us to ascertain our level of comprehension and inquired, "Is that clear?"

George could not help himself, "Why must we discuss inadequate theories that are obviously missing important information that we know to be true?"

Agnes frowned, slapped the top of her desk, and responded, "Because that is what we call science!" She shook her head in disgust, took a moment to regather her composure, and asked rhetorically, "Now where was I? Oh, yes! This is where the Novikov self-consistency principle comes in. It essentially tells us that any changes in history were changes that were already destined to occur. In other words, everything that happens is already meant to happen. Ultimately, the presence of a Time Traveler has no impact upon a fixed timeline."

She looked out upon the class and provided us with an idea for further contemplation, "Think about the course of history contained within the ATL— the approved timeline. This is history as it is supposed to occur. The fixed timeline theory principle suggests that the work we are doing has had no impact upon time— we are simply ensuring the inevitable."

She nodded, adding as an afterthought, "The Novikov principal also presents the idea that either there is only one timeline, or if there are alternate timelines, they are not accessible to anyone other than an individual who already resides upon that timeline."

George spoke only loud enough for me to understand his words, "Someone should tell this to Emmett."

Agnes turned to look in our direction, but she appeared uncertain as to what he had actually said. "George, do you have something to say?" she inquired.

"No Ma'am."

Although appearing unconvinced, she replied nonetheless, "Very well." She then pointed toward the second set of words on the board, "Let us examine the idea of time travel within a dynamic timeline . . . It might be easiest to simply understand this kind of time travel as one filled with paradoxes!"

"Paradox time travel," Emanuel volunteered from his seat.

"Exactly!" Agnes agreed wholeheartedly. "This theory suggests that even changing your past, present, and future is possible with time travel! No doubt you remember the grandfather paradox from your first semester?"

"No doubt," George replied softly.

"Imagine you go back and accidentally kill your grandfather in his youth, thereby preventing your own birth in your grandfather's future . . . if you were never born, how could you go back in time to kill your grandfather?"

"It is a paradox," Manuela agreed.

"Time travel in a dynamic timeline creates all kinds of paradoxes because altered events in the past have an impact upon anything that occurs thereafter . . . Once the past has been changed, a ripple in time moves forward and changes everything in its path."

Emanuel questioned aloud, "Madame, is this problem not addressed by the existence of multiple timelines?"

Our instructress frowned for having been interrupted yet again in the middle of her instruction, but she continued regardless, "Let's not too quickly move past the dynamic timeline theory." She waved the stylus in Emanuel's direction and reminded him, "Although it may not be common knowledge among proponents of the dynamic timeline theory, just as the League facility exists out of time, a Time Traveler would remain untouched by any changes that occurred in the past. Time would change around that Wayfarer." She added for our clarification, "Obviously, the individual could not go back to a personal past after the point of change, because it would no longer exist on a dynamic timeline."

"Évidemment . . . obviously," Bonne Soeur Marie voiced aloud.

"Good," Agnes nodded, "That brings us to alternate timelines and the multiverse theory of time travel . . ."

"Thank, God," George said a little too loudly. Agnes stared angrily in his direction, but George quickly added, "This is my favorite part!"

"I see," her response sounded dubious. "In any event, the multiverse theory suggests that each timeline—each universe—is just one of many . . ."

I decided to participate in the discussion and volunteered, "Like the many timelines we find ourselves shepherding."

"Exactly!" our instructress agreed. "There are many timelines. However, what makes this theory somewhat confusing is it suggests that whenever you make a change to your own timeline, you somehow push yourself out of that timeline and suddenly find yourself in another." Agnes paused and reflected upon her words before adding, "Obviously, scientists who ascribe to this theory have never had the opportunity to use a Horologium."

George mouthed the word, "Obviously," but he said nothing.

Agnes continued, "What may be most interesting about this theory is that in the 1950s a student at Princeton named Hugh Everett theorized that every time an individual made a choice or a decision, or took one direction over another, another timeline was created. He believed that ultimately there were infinite timelines and infinite variables of yourself. Isn't that amazing?"

Agnes looked around the room hoping for a broader sense of amazement but when she found none, she simply shook her head in disappointment. "Any thoughts?" she asked finally.

It was George who finally replied, "Sounds like the Akasha library to me."

Emanuel added, "Definitely, the Akasha."

Our instructress shook her head, placed her stylus upon the desk, and conceded, "I think you have had enough enlightenment for one evening . . . Class dismissed!"

George turned to me and demanded, "Meet me in our room. I need to get out of here in case Louise is waiting for me."

A moment later, he was gone.

It was while walking alone in the direction of my chambers that the sound of footsteps and the rich scent of French perfume came to my senses. A soft hand reached out and touched my shoulder. I turned to see Louise #217 standing behind me.

Louise sighed, "Ben, I need to ask you a question." She paused as if to consider how best to phrase the query. She chose the most straightforward approach, "Are you absolutely certain that George likes women?"

Her stunning appearance did not go unnoticed, and I struggled to keep my mind on the question at hand. I cleared my throat before speaking, "Yes, Louise. I am most certain he likes women."

She appeared unconvinced, "How can you be sure? I made my intentions quite obvious."

A thought escaped me, "You are a most formidable woman."

Her lips frowned slightly, "How do you know he likes women?"

I recollected myself and replied, "He was engaged once, and very much in love." I spoke with certainty.

"What was her name?"

It took but a moment to recall one of our earliest conversations. I answered, "Her name was Esther . . . Esther Hoppin, I believe. George told me that she was from a wealthy family in Rhode Island. She journeyed to London to be present for the coronation of Victoria.

It was there they met, through mutual friends. George told me that he found himself smitten from the very first."

Louise appeared confused, "What happened?"

"Esther broke it off. She fell in love with another man and chose to marry him instead. She married a banker." I looked at Louise and admitted that which I thought to be true, "I think George was so hurt by what happened that he swore never to love again. Since then, his focus has been philanthropy."

Louise pondered my words for several moments, nodded her head, and informed me, "I need to change my approach."

I replied without thinking, "That would be most helpful for all concerned."

"Pardon?" She looked at me inquisitively.

"I think that is a very good idea."

I quickly begged my leave and proceeded to return to my room, forcing myself not to glance back in her direction.

No one within the League or even the Core that governs it can speak with authority as to how long this work will be ours to perform. Although this simple recognition appears easy to comprehend, it can be bitter to experience. In truth, the seemingly eternal nature of our efforts has long been cited as the cause by those who have chosen to leave this work behind. For this reason, rather than focusing on the end result, it is perhaps more advantageous to become fixated on whatever task is before you.

It is a certainty that no one has the means to bring our goal to quick fruition. No one possesses the ability to decide the swiftest approach for attaining that which we ultimately desire. After a great deal of personal effort and more time since the first moment of my involvement than I might have imagined at the start, I have chosen to understand our efforts as an ongoing process rather than as any solitary goal. My counsel to every Wayfarer is simply this: remain focused on the process.

Excerpt, "Preface," *Wayfarer's Manual — Continuing Education (revised edition);* **by Ruth #7**

SIX: Journal Entry — January 11 ATL

I believe George has finally decided to forgive me for my involvement in the Louise situation. To be sure, on two occasions he has reminded me that "under no circumstance" am I to initiate a plan that attempts to establish an arrangement between himself and any individual of the female gender. He has stated unequivocally, "I am my own man, and do not require your help!" As a means of continuing our friendship and returning to the agreeable relationship we have shared thus far, I have given him my word that I will never again instigate a similar situation. However, I remain steadfast in my resolve to watch for an opportunity that might arise in which someone else chooses to execute a plan of their own in this regard. Should that occur, I see no reason not to render my assistance.

In the midst of our various discussions, George did volunteer the fact that he had been somewhat frightened by Louise's insistent advances. Her new approach (which I have indeed witnessed at various mealtimes) appears to be one of providing him with unconditional support while waiting for him to make the first move. I believe she is hopeful that this will lead to, what might be called, the natural course of events in this business of male-female relations. For my part, however, I find myself thankful that neither we nor the League facility are bound by time, as these tactics may prove quite prolonged in their successful execution.

Setting aside the George and Louise situation, I should confess that ever since Athena first suggested our collective timeline mission assignments were nothing more than a diversion, I have been unable to commit myself to our work with the same level of personal dedication. In fact, it has been somewhat challenging of late for me to maintain my heretofore enthusiasm and focus, knowing that we may simply be participants in what Athena now refers to as "a Core-created distraction."

It was during the course of one of those days when the thoughts of George, Louise, and the ongoing intrigue regarding the Core itself frequently took turns running through my mind that a most usual occurrence took place. Without a doubt, the experience provided me with some clarity as to the reason why Agnes seems most prone to a measure of theatrical excess during each of her classroom presentations.

As background information (as George might verbally assert), in our supposed search for Emmett, each of us Wayfarers had just been provided with yet another timeline assignment from the ATL Mission Office. We were informed that our collective goal remained very much the same. We were to return to a historical event with which we have some semblance of familiarity and investigate our assigned timeline as a possible duplicate of the ATL. If the timeline was identical to our previous recollection (or at least a very close proximity), we were to report it to the mission office immediately. Once these parameters had been communicated yet again by Milton #71, I received the assignment of timeline XCVI.

Although I briefly considered a return to the Roosevelt White House, as the personalities of Churchill, the President, and the First Lady remain quite appealing to me, I reflected upon some of my more notable travel missions and decided it might be best to visit a different locale while the details still remained fresh in my mind. It was that impetus that led me back to Mali, Africa, and a second encounter with Sundiata Keita, one of the continent's most important rulers and the creator of the Manden Charter.

I recalled the charter as being an oral composition of human rights that Keita had originated. After its creation, it was passed down through verbal presentation and dramatic oration for generations until it was finally written down. Much like the Greek tradition of oral poetry that had given birth to the *Iliad* and *Odyssey* 2,000 years earlier, with Athena's assistance, I learned that Africa possessed its own heritage of orature—a method of spoken and musical performances that related important facts, history, and culture that were important to its people.

I set aside all thoughts of George, Louise, and the Core, and made a return journey to Africa while keeping my musings of the king and his city in the forefront of my mind. Not long thereafter, I found myself in Sundiata Keita's personal chambers, standing within the king himself. As is most common in these targeted arrivals, my own ghostly extremities moved in vaporous motion around and through him. He stood in colorful robes before his three sons (Wali, Ouati, and Khalifa), reflecting aloud upon the duties of a ruler toward his subjects.

I listened as he gave voice to the importance of both compassion and justice. The king's words were very much like those I remembered, and the feeling I got from his personage was identical to how I had felt about Keita during my previous encounter. I listened long enough to ascertain that this was, in all likelihood, another possibility that needed to be passed along to the ATL Mission Office. As the king continued his discussion, I used my Wayfarer's influence to separate myself from him and suddenly recalled aloud (though no one could hear me), "This is when I saw Emmett."

I turned to look where the old man had stood previously and noticed an open window within Keita's chamber. Through the opening, I could hear the distant sounds of music and the Mandinka language. As Emmett was nowhere to be seen, I walked forward and peered out into the city street below, which lay several stories beneath me.

A large crowd had gathered outside the king's fortress and was beginning to separate themselves, like parting waters, in order to allow a group of three African oratures to sing, dance, and entertain their way through the crowd. The performance consisted of two men and a woman, with one man tapping a drum and the other playing a small stringed instrument. The woman moved about dramatically as she gave voice to the oration of her tale. I immediately caught my breath with surprise upon taking a second glance at the woman below.

"It's Agnes!" I spoke aloud.

She led the other performers, frequently bobbing about as she alternated between singing and speaking in rhyme. She waved her arms before her, pointing in the direction of one member of the crowd and then another as if she held a stylus before them (though there was no stylus to be found). Her colorful robes twirled and spun about with her movements, keeping in time with the music and her rhythmic speech. She hopped and jumped and twirled before the people of Mali with more flair than seemed required for such an oration. To be sure, I knew what I was witnessing had occurred prior to her own recruitment into the League. For a time, I was unable to direct my eyes elsewhere.

As I watched the performance capture the complete attention of all those who stood nearby, I could not help but smile.

"She has not changed in the least," I said only to myself.

During our next scheduled required continuing education seminar, I watched Agnes with renewed interest. She bobbed about before us, moving in front of the whiteboard as she dramatically pointed the stylus in one direction and then another. For a brief instant, I almost perceived the colorful robes spinning about her. If nothing else, her classroom performances were consistent.

After my return to the League, I dutifully reported timeline XCVI as a possible location for Emmett. Obviously, Athena and I remained very much aware that had the timeline truly been a possibility, it would not have been assigned in the first place. In addition to myself, Emanuel also reported his timeline assignment as a potential alternate. After everyone reported (and ignoring what other Time Travelers beyond our group might be accomplishing), that brought the remainder on Grimwald's listing to 2,847. Although I truly wanted to inform my fellow Wayfarers that these missions were little more than a distraction, I could not yet take the chance as such knowledge might expose us to whatever member of the Core was working with Emmett.

While in the midst of such musings, I heard a loud bang, just as Agnes slapped her hand on top of her desk. The noise was startling, causing me to jump in my seat.

I looked up to see her pointing the stylus in my direction. She spoke with frustration, "Ben! Have you been listening?"

"Ma'am?" was the solitary word that escaped me.

Agnes sighed, "I asked you to describe the plot of the book, *Hands Off*. What were your thoughts about it?"

I could not help but be confused, "Ma'am?"

Our instructress shook her head in annoyance, "It was part of your assigned reading in the text."

A look of bewilderment undoubtedly crossed my face as she continued, "The Wayfarer's Manual text!" She looked around the class and inquired, "Does anyone wish to tell me their thoughts on the reading assignment?"

Immediately, Emanuel and Bonne Soeur Marie raised a hand in the air. Agnes pointed the stylus at Emanuel.

Our Swede scholar spoke with certainty, "Madame Agnes, both the story and its title, 'Hands Off' present the possible risks and uncertainties one might encounter when changing history through time travel. Such endeavors must always be approached with caution."

Ages nodded approvingly, "Anything else?"

Emanuel continued, "Well, we know this is the story of a Time Traveler . . ."

"How do we know that?" George interrupted, sounding unconvinced.

Emanuel was not to be deterred, "From the text! In the first sentence, the main character tells the reader — and I quote — 'I was in another existence . . . free from the limits of time.' Obviously, he is a Wayfarer."

My roomie was unmoved, "It's a fictional story by a man named Edward Hale. It has no basis in fact."

Agnes spoke next, "Can you be so certain, George?"

George replied matter of fact, "Very certain."

"Any other thoughts?" she looked about the classroom.

Manuela #64 responded, "I believe it is true. The main character refers to the person accompanying him as 'this guardian of mine.' Isn't such a person his recruiter, from the League?"

"Good point," Agnes nodded approvingly.

I kept my eyes focused forward, not knowing what to say. Unfortunately, our instructress appeared determined to refocus her attention back in my direction.

"Did everyone except Ben read the assignment?"

I looked around the room and saw Manuela, George, Bonne Soeur, and Emanuel, each nodding in the affirmative.

"I was busy on a timeline mission," came my justification.

Agnes was not impressed, "So was everyone else!" She shook her head in annoyance, "Let me tell you what you were supposed to read." She proceeded to the board and wrote the words "Joseph, son of Jacob" before us, underlined them twice, and inquired, "I assume you are familiar with the name?"

"I am," I replied. "In the Old Testament, he is one of Jacob's twelve sons, the favorite. Because his brothers are jealous, they sell him into slavery. He ends up in Egypt, where it is discovered that he can interpret dreams. That talent served him well as the pharaoh has a dream that disturbs him greatly."

Agnes motioned in my direction, "Continue."

"Pharaoh dreamed that seven fat cows came out of the Nile. These fat cows were followed close behind by seven skinny cows, and the second set of cows proceeded to eat the first. Joseph interprets the dream to mean that Egypt will have seven years of plenty followed by seven years of famine, and the country needs to prepare for what is to come. Pharaoh believed the interpretation and put Joseph in charge of all preparations. Because of his actions, Egypt survived the famine."

"Apparently you found time to read that version of the story!" she said with a measure of irritation. "In our assigned reading, you would have read that our main character goes back in time and helps Joseph escape from slavery. As a result, he never gets to Egypt, and he never interprets Pharaoh's dream." She slapped the top of her desk for emphasis, "That changes history! The people of Egypt starve, and the Egyptian empire comes to an end. That one act by one Time Traveler changes the world!"

Bonne Soeur Marie was quick to reply, "Ç'est bien . . . It is good in the end. The man's recruiter resets time, just the way it is supposed to be."

"It's a fictional story!" George insisted. "It is not about a real Time Traveler!"

"Are you sure?" Agnes replied with conviction. "In any event," she turned to point the stylus in my direction, "Assigned reading is to be read when it is assigned! Understood?"

"Yes, Ma'am."

"Good." She nodded her head in approval and proceeded to take a folded piece of paper out of her dress pocket. She spoke with enthusiasm, "You will all be very pleased to hear that I have your most recent business-as-usual travel assignments from the ATL Mission Office!"

George could not help but reply, "You have got to be kidding!"

Agnes frowned at him momentarily before quickly turning her head to read from the paper:

"Emanuel #41, destination Chitpur, West Bengal, 1830, in the matter of Raja Rammohan Roy and his commitment to the Indian Renaissance and Hindu reforms."

"Manuela #64, destination Lagos, Nigeria, 2112, in the matter of Adaku Musa and her work on income inequality for the people."

"George #111, destination Dublin, Ireland, 2029, in the matter of Rory Gallagher and the expansion of the Ireland Funds Foundation."

"Ben #239, destination London, England, 1940, in the matter of Nora Baker and her efforts with the French resistance."

"Bonne Soeur Marie #304, destination Cleveland, Ohio, 2038, in the matter of Dr. Samja Talreja and AI advancements in robotic surgery."

Agnes waved the sheet of paper before us while providing her usual recommendation, "You will want to visit Athena in the library for assistance with these assignments. Athena knows everything!"

While Athena was occupied, assisting my fellow Wayfarers in the Akasha library with their own mission assignments, I spent an hour researching Nora Baker on my own. What I learned proved to be an unusual combination of the inspirational, the intriguing, and the surprising.

To begin, Nora Baker was not her real name; she was born Noor Inayat Khan. In an earlier era, she would have been a princess, as she descended from seventeenth-century Indian royalty. The daughter of a Sufi preacher/musician, Hazrat Inayat Khan, and an American, Ora Ray Baker, her parents met in California. Her father often traveled, providing audiences with Sufi philosophy, music, or even both. The couple married in London but soon moved to Moscow, where Noor was born. Because of the threat of the Great War (World War I), the family emigrated to England, where three additional children eventually arrived—all sons. In 1920, the family resettled in France, which is where Noor and her brothers grew up. They were fluent in both English and French.

The Khan home was called a "House of Blessings." Music, creativity, and the acceptance of every faith were encouraged. Noor's father rejected violence and prejudice, urging his children to do the same. He also championed the principle of always assisting those in need, reminding his children, "There are occasions when great service demands great sacrifice." Although he died when Noor was only 13, each of his offspring remained influenced by his philosophy for the remainder of their lives. Noor studied at the Sorbonne and began a career writing stories for children. She published her first book in 1939 when she was 25.

When Germany invaded France in May 1940, Noor's family moved back to England. Four months later, the German bombing of England began, and Noor and her brother, Vilayat, vowed to find a way to help England. Vilayat volunteered for the Royal Air Force (RAF) and Noor volunteered for the Women's Auxiliary Air Force (WAAF), where she became one of the first women trained in communication for what was described as "wireless radio," specializing in something called Morse code. In that very capacity, Noor decided to take the name "Nora," hoping to fit in with the other women and lessen any objection to her Indian heritage. She also adopted her mother's family name, "Baker." This was the extent of my research when Athena finally made an appearance at the table, offering her assistance.

"What can I do to help you?"

I looked up with a big smile. She looked at me knowingly, and smiled in return, "Besides a shaking of the sheets, what can I do to help?"

I nodded, "My mission overview is quite clear; I need to make certain this Nora Baker joins the French resistance. I have yet to ascertain, however, the challenge that stands in the way of such an outcome."

"Give me a little time to research the matter, and I will return."

While my beloved engaged herself elsewhere, I continued to examine the information within several volumes that lay scattered on the table before me. I soon learned that Prime Minister Churchill's office established a war effort called the SOE—the Special Operation Executive. Its mission was to conduct sabotage and espionage against the Germans while providing assistance to resistance efforts throughout Europe. I also discovered that Nora's proficiency with Morse code was flawless. Due to her wireless skills and her competence in French and English, within two years she came to the attention of the SOE. She was called to a meeting at their organizational offices within the Victoria Hotel. When they first approached her, she had never even heard of the SOE.

According to the text I had procured, during her first interview, the SOE told Nora that she was being considered for training as a special agent to be sent to France for undercover work. They admitted the work would be quite dangerous. While there, she would have no protection from the British government, and she would be immediately shot by the Germans if she was caught. Without hesitation, Nora said she wanted the assignment.

It was in the midst of exploring the SOE training process (which included fake Gestapo interviews, a series of athletic exercises, advice for remaining undercover, and the like) that Athena returned. As I peered up from the volume I had been reading, it was immediately apparent that she was troubled.

"Is there a problem with the assignment?" I inquired.

Athena shook her head, "No, not the assignment. As far as the Akasha is concerned your task is straightforward enough. On multiple timelines, her brother brings to mind their father's pacifism and talks Nora out of joining the SOE. Somehow that creates Allied problems for D-Day. You need to make certain that Nora follows her heart and joins the resistance."

"Then what's the problem?"

Athena's words were somber, "At the time, there was a great deal of discrimination against Indian nationals. Although the Akasha indicates Nora's work was important to the resistance, it also suggests certain members of the SOE considered an alternate plan that led to her capture."

I was astonished, "For what purpose?"

"If it became necessary, they would purposefully send Nora false information. After acquiring Allied information that was not true, her identity would be revealed so that she would be arrested. Once captured and tortured, she would inevitably pass that propaganda onto the Germans, providing them with distorted facts about Allied plans.

I found myself disgusted by such duplicity but inquired nonetheless, "What is the actual history according to the ATL?"

"Her service is extremely important to both England and France," came her reply. "For a time, she will be the only wireless operator still undercover, receiving and transmitting important operation details for the SOE. She will be betrayed by a member of the French resistance and taken into custody. After being imprisoned, chained, and beaten, she will be transported to the Dachau concentration camp. There she will be repeatedly tortured and interrogated. She will reveal nothing about the resistance, nor will she provide any names."

As I looked at my beloved, it became apparent that her eyes had become quite moist. She continued, "One night, she will be kicked and beaten until she collapses in exhaustion. Afterward, she will be shot in the back of the head by a member of the SS. Through it all, Nora will reveal nothing . . . not one single word." Athena sighed before adding, "Four years after the war, the British government will award her the George Cross for gallantry."

Not long thereafter, I took Horologium in hand and proceeded to undertake the necessary steps to travel to my assignment—one Noor Inayat Khan. After experiencing a relatively brief fall, I soon found that my body had taken on the appearance of its ghostly self, continually moving in swirls of motion through each of my target's extremities. As is often the case in these Time Travel experiences, it took a moment to collect my Wayfarer thoughts and use such influence to separate myself from my target. Once accomplished, I found myself staring at Nora and her brother, Vilayat, standing before me.

My immediate impression of the pair was that they were both kind and gentle. Although it quickly became apparent that there was disagreement between them, neither raised a voice toward the other. Each remained thoughtful when listening and considerate while speaking. The combined heritage of their parents had provided the siblings with good looks, for the two possessed large and engaging eyes, hair that was a shade of ebony, and a skin tone tinted like a perfect cup of coffee with cream (or perhaps a piece of the most delicious caramel). Vilayat was speaking, while his sister listened until he had finished. It was then that she gently shook her head and disagreed.

"This is something I must do," she said calmly. "Indians need to win distinction in this war. If only one or two can do something truly brave, they will be admired by the English, and it will help bring the people of England and the people of India together."

I was reminded of what I had read but a brief time before—she would change her name to fit in with the others. She possessed a desire to be accepted.

"Noor . . . Noor," he repeated her name, "I fear you will find it impossible to serve both your country and your religion. In the end, you will need to betray one or the other."

"I will betray neither," she asserted. "I love England, and I hold to the faith of our father."

His words were somber, "They will give you a gun."

"I cannot kill. I will refuse to use it."

"Noor, you may not have a choice. You will not have a choice! Europe is at war. In the end, I worry you will either kill or be killed." He looked upon her with compassion, "This is not the way to nonviolence. This is not the way of Mahatma. This is not the way of our father. Why does it have to be you?"

She contemplated his words and stated what quickly came to mind, "I know Paris better than most Englishmen. I must do something."

Vilayat reached out and grasped her hand in his own, saying, "Together, let us find some other way to help. There will be another way."

As she looked at him and considered his words, I knew that the moment of her hesitation had arrived. I immediately took Horologium in hand and decided to revisit the timeline a few moments before. After the sensation of a quick leap, in an instant I found myself revisiting the repetition of her name.

"Noor . . . Noor," Vilayat said calmly, "I fear you may find it impossible to serve both your country and your religion. In the end, you will need to betray one or the other."

Using my Wayfarer's influences, I drew upon Nora's own deep frustration, and allowed her to reply, "I will betray neither," she asserted. "I love England, and I hold to the faith of our father. I need to be more than a WAAF. Somehow, I need to be of greater help."

"But they will give you a gun," he said gravely.
"I cannot kill. I will refuse to use it."
"Noor, you may not have a choice. You will not
have a choice! Europe is at war. In the end, I worry you
will either kill or be killed." He looked upon her with
compassion, "This is not the way to nonviolence. This
is not the way of Mahatma. This is not the way of our
father. Why does it have to be you?"
She was not moved in the least, "I know Paris better
than most Englishmen. I must do something."
"I still do not understand." He shook his head in
defeat, "What would father say to this?"
She contemplated his words for a moment and
replied, "He would say, 'There come occasions when
great service demands great sacrifice.' That is what he
would say, and this is what I must do."
He reached out to grasp her hand within his own, "Is
there not some other way to help?"
She repeated, "This is what I must do."
After her words had been spoken, I quickly made the
journey home. I found that I possessed a real appreciation
for this woman and had no desire to remain witness to
that which was to come.

Each of the others had already finished describing
their latest mission assignments, and I had chosen
to go last. I had begun my tale by admitting that the
mission was one of those that had been accomplished
successfully but in which there had been absolutely
no satisfaction in the outcome. I provided my fellow
Wayfarers with the essential points I had learned
within the library as well as those I had experienced

firsthand with Nora, including the final conversation between she and her brother. After taking the last bite of my muffin and sipping the remainder of my coffee, I chose to end the tale by briefly describing what had come next.

"Early one morning, the other women at the WAAF learned that Nora had simply disappeared. She had no conversation with any of her coworkers, and she left behind no note. She had simply folded her blanket and left it on her bed. Her career in the SOE secret service began. Nora became the first female wireless operator to be sent from England into occupied France to help the French Resistance. She was given the codename 'Madeleine.'"

Bonne Soeur Marie interrupted, "Vivre libre ou mourir . . . live free or die."

I nodded and ended with a final postscript, "Although the SOE had issued Nora a gun and cyanide capsules for her mission, she had left both behind. She refused to take any life, even her own. She died on September 13, 1944, when she was only 30 years old."

Each of the others appeared moved by the story, and there seemed little that could be said in response to such a tale. Afterward, our mealtime camaraderie came to an end. A moment later, I kissed my beloved Athena and said my goodbyes to George and the others. I knew that Athena was headed for the library and George said he would see me later in our chambers. I was standing just outside the League Café doorway when I saw Ruth #7 heading in my direction down the long hallway.

"Do you have a moment?" I inquired when she was within arm's length.

Her youthful visage looked upon me with those intense, sparkling eyes. She said only, "Absolutely."

I nodded approvingly, "I have been wanting to inquire if you ever saw Emmett back at the Roosevelt White House?"

She appeared startled and it took her a moment before offering a reply, "What are you talking about?"

I responded, "Remember when we were with Sara and Milton discussing the situation with Emmett? You told us you were going to try and discover how Emmett knew I was going to have an unusual experience with Churchill during my Eleanor Roosevelt mission?"

She continued to look confused but recalled nonetheless, "I remember."

"I was just wondering if you saw anything?"

Ruth's look of bewilderment continued, prompting me to ask outright, "When I saw you on my mission to the Roosevelt White House, did you ever see Emmett?"

She watched me intensely, until finally speaking words that disturbed me greatly.

"Ben, I have never been to the Roosevelt White House."

Undoubtedly, your education and your own timeline experiences will have acquainted you with a greater understanding of the collective Consciousness that existed within all of Creation prior to Moment One. Ever since the beginning of time's passage, the reattainment of that Consciousness has been the primary goal of the Core, the League, and the work with which we are all involved. It is a Consciousness we might imagine, even though our own perceptions of its possibilities remain fleeting at best.

In reality, consciousness only grows and expands; it does not diminish. While age and the frailties of the human mind can appear to minimize the capacity of thought, individual consciousness is not subject to the same weaknesses. Perhaps it is time then for you to consider a most extraordinary hypothesis. For that reason, I offer you this: If consciousness is incapable of decline, why do we perceive that which existed before Moment One as being lost? Why do we undertake travels through history to expand a consciousness that has never been absent? How long must it be before we reawaken to that which has always been true? Is it possible that all of our perceived experiences are little more than an illusion in personal consciousness? Think, think on these things.

Excerpt, "Understanding the Nature of Time Travel," *Wayfarer's Manual — Continuing Education (revised edition);* **by Ruth #7**

SEVEN: *Journal Entry — January 17 ATL*

Although nearly a week had passed since my conversation with Ruth #7 in the hallway, I had been unable to completely free myself from the worry that frequently returned to my mind. Since that time, my thoughts had dwelt upon the unthinkable. It had been rather difficult to allow my heretofore rational self to embrace the one inevitable conclusion that repeatedly came before me, but it was one that Ruth herself had voiced within the hallway.

"Somehow, Emmett has recruited my duplicate." Her words had been spoken softly so that only I could hear. They were quickly followed by a demand, "We can tell no one."

I momentarily considered requesting an exception to such a stance but promptly arrived at the same conclusion. For the time being (and until we knew more), it was best to keep such knowledge between ourselves. When the occasion arose, I would suggest that we needed to bring Athena into our confidence. Perhaps my beloved could be of some assistance in the matter.

After Ruth's declaration, I took the opportunity to inquire what she had meant when she informed the Governor-General and me that she would look into the matter of how Emmett could know about the Eleanor Roosevelt mission before it had even been assigned.

"If you were not going to look for Emmett yourself, what did you plan to do?"

Ruth replied, "I went to see Athena. Together, we examined dozens of timelines in the library. Even then it became quite clear that what Emmett claimed to see in his version of the Akasha library was not possible."

"Someone within the facility must have told him about the mission before it was announced."

She nodded, "That is the only conclusion."

A thought came to mind which I spoke aloud, "Can we be so certain that he has created another Akasha?"

Ruth was confident, "We can. He needs to have an Akasha if he has any hope of replacing the ATL." She then took her own Horologium and held it in her hand before me. "Do you remember when you first got here, and the CORE was tracking my Horologium, which Emmett had stolen?"

"I certainly do! You can track a Horologium when someone makes a change to the timeline."

"Yes," she concurred, "but soon after Emmett disappeared, we tried to use the Akasha to find him, but had no success. Even when he was changing history, his whereabouts remained unknown."

I had yet to fully understand what she was suggesting, "What does that mean?"

"It means he is no longer connected to our Akasha but to his own. That is why we have been unable to find him."

Soon after our conversation had come to an end, a second notion came to the forefront of my mind. How was it even possible that I would encounter Ruth's duplicate at the very moment I was in the White House on that specific timeline? Considering the infinite possibilities of timelines and potential moments within each, the chances of such an occurrence happening on its own bordered on the impossible. These were the cogitations that held my attention when Agnes's voice suddenly intruded and pushed all other thoughts aside.

"Ben, are you even listening?" She demanded loudly, pointing the stylus in my direction.

I found the presence of mind to respond, "Yes, ma'am."

She looked at me with skepticism, "Really? What was I saying?"

Out of the corner of my eye, I could see three underlined words written on the board before me. I quickly voiced them aloud, "The Nechtansmere Time Slip."

She frowned but nodded in response, "Very well. Let me begin with some background information on the Battle of Nechtansmere."

"Why not?" George whispered just under his breath. Agnes had apparently heard nothing as she turned back to the board and wrote the word "Picts," underlining it twice, followed by the word "Northumbrians," which was underlined in the same manner.

She turned to us and spoke with certainty, "Now these are the facts! In the seventh century, there was a battle between the Picts and the Northumbrians. The Picts were early descendants of the native inhabitants of Scotland." She turned in the direction of Emanuel and provided the following, "You might be interested to learn that the Romans themselves referred to these people as 'Picti,' as they loved to cover themselves with blue, fierce-looking tattoos, making them appear quite frightening in battle. The Picts were led by King Bridei Mac Bili." She dutifully recorded his name on the board.

She wrote a second name as she continued, "The Northumbrians were led by King Ecgfrith," and then turned back to exclaim, "You might be interested to learn that these two kings were cousins!" She shook her head in disbelief and stated, "Unbelievable! In any event, the battle took place on May 20, 685, as it is recorded on the ATL ..."

George interrupted, "What was the battle about?"

Our instructress looked at him curiously, seemingly pondering whether he truly wanted an answer, or if desired simply to interrupt. She frowned slightly but responded nonetheless, "For years, the Northumbrians had dominated the region but that came to an end when Bridei decided that his people needed additional land."

Agnes nodded in agreement with her own words and provided an aside, "You see, the Picts were mostly farmers, raising crops of oats, barley, rye, and such. They also herded sheep, pigs, and cattle. Obviously, you need land for those kinds of activities."

"What about the time slip?" George interrupted again.

Agnes slapped the top of her desk with her hand, "I am getting to that . . . Now where were we?"

Bonne Soeur Marie volunteered, "You were talking about King Bridei taking land for his people."

"Exactly!" Agnes waved the stylus in Soeur Marie's direction. "The last thing I need to tell you . . ." she turned back to George, "because it is important to the time slip, is that these people used resin from the Scottish fir tree in their torches. That type of resin burn reds. In any event, the last battle took place somewhere around Dunnichen Hill, near a lake that has long since disappeared. During the fighting, Ecgfrith, the Northumbrian king, was killed."

George immediately lifted his hand in the air, prompting Agnes to point the stylus in his direction. Her words were firm, "That is all you need to know for the purpose of this discussion! Let's talk about the time slip."

Agnes took only a moment to recollect her thoughts before continuing, "The Nechtansmere Time Slip occurred in January 1950. A 55-year-old woman by the name of Elizabeth Smith — she liked to be called 'Liz' — was driving her car at night in the middle of a rainstorm along a dirt road with her little dog, Perry . . ."

George quickly inquired, "What kind of dog was it?"

Our instructress was not pleased with the query, "It is not relevant to our discussion! In any event, she had just left the city of Brechin and was headed back to her own small village called Letham, which is near Dunnichen Hill. It was dark and it was raining. Suddenly, her vehicle started skidding through the mud and the car ended up in a ditch!"

As a means of providing us with a theatrical component to the tale, Agnes positioned her hands, as if she were driving a car, and suddenly jerked her body completely upright to illustrate coming to an abrupt and sudden stop.

Her narration continued, "As it was unlikely anyone else would be coming along the road at that time of night, Liz decided she needed to walk to the nearest home and ask for help. She picked up her dog and started walking down the roadway, which was nothing more than a muddy trail. A short time later, the rain stopped, and Liz could see lights off in the distance." Our instructress squinted her eyes as if looking far away, "She soon realized that the lights were moving closer."

Agnes stopped speaking and looked at us, one at a time. First George, then me, then Emanuel, followed by Manuela, and finally Bonne Soeur Marie. After taking time to peer upon each one of us in turn, she remained silent.

Finally, it was Manuela #64 who asked impatiently, "What happened next?"

"Just making certain that everyone is listening!" Our instructress nodded approvingly, "Apparently, that little dog, Perry, started to growl. Liz grabbed the dog's snout so he would remain silent." Agnes demonstrated such with her own hands. "As the lights grew closer, they appeared to be flickering flames that gave off the color red. Liz realized they were torches—dozens of them. She noticed that rather than coming straight toward her, the flames were moving in an elongated direction, as if the torches were being carried around

a rather large circle. A few moments later, she could
see that the flames were being carried by the shadowy
figures of more than a hundred men. They continued to
move closer."

"Avait-elle peur?" Bonne Soeur Marie asked, and
then again, "Was she afraid?"

"At first," Agnes concurred, "but even when the
warriors came near, they didn't seem to see her standing
there in the shadows. Instead, they were occupied with
their search, bending down, and inspecting countless
bodies that had suddenly appeared on the ground.
They turned over one fallen warrior after another, as if
looking for anyone who might still be alive. Liz stood
quietly, watching this process for the longest time until
all of the warriors had finally passed her by."

Our teacher digressed, "Let me tell you, it was quite
a while before she made it home that night. She soon
told her experience to her neighbors, most of whom
weren't certain what to believe. You see, although the
experience was most unusual, Liz had a reputation of
being quite practical and down to earth." Agnes shook
her stylus and insisted, "She was certainly not prone
to fantasy! It wasn't long before her story got out, and
she was interviewed by both a psychologist and a
researcher. They didn't believe her at first, but it was
later discovered that a lake had once existed exactly
where Elizabeth claimed the shadowy figures had been
forced to walk, as if going around a large circle. After
that, both interviewers came to believe the tale."

Our instructress slapped the top of her desk for
emphasis, "That is the Nechtansmere Time Slip! Are
there any questions?"

George chose to ask, "What happened to the dog?"

Agnes ignored him, shook her head in dismay, and
proceeded to pull a folded piece of paper out of her

dress pocket, "You will be very pleased to learn that the ATL Mission Office has given me new timelines for your ongoing all-hands-on-deck assignments. It is time to go looking for Emmett!"

In the end, it was an appreciation for Churchill and the Roosevelts that prompted my decision to make a quick return to the White House. As these assignments were little more than diversions, there was no reason why I couldn't enjoy myself in the process. I chose as my target none other than Franklin Delano Roosevelt himself and decided to arrive on December 31, 1941. My assignment was timeline XVIII.

During my previous journey, that particular evening had been one of hope and laughter, and an amusing movie titled "The Man Who Came to Dinner" had held the attention of all present. In fact, to everyone's delight, Eleanor's voice was a surprise feature at the end of the program (they called it "a cameo"). Unfortunately, I had been so focused on remaining watchful for Emmett that I had missed out on much of the merriment. I planned to correct that on my subsequent expedition.

I arrived that morning in the Oval Office and found myself sitting within the figure of the President himself. He sat behind his desk as he spoke to Undersecretary of War Robert Patterson and Bernard Baruch, financier, industrialist, and a close personal advisor. Apparently, Baruch had helped to mobilize various companies and industries during the Great War and had been recruited to do much the same during this most recent conflict.

Roosevelt was quick to the point, "At no time has the security of our country been as threatened as it is today." "Understood, Mr. President," Mr. Baruch replied, and then spoke with certainty, "I have every confidence that we can redirect the business of industry to the business of war. We will give the War Department everything it needs to win this thing. It will take time, but it can be done."

The Undersecretary interjected, "Mr. Baruch has a proposal for shortening the entire production schedule for tanks and aircraft."

Roosevelt was intrigued. He leaned forward and inquired, "Is that possible?"

"It is possible," Baruch assured him. "Our first priority will be retooling the factories. While that occurs, we need to redirect gasoline, materials, food, and supplies toward the entire war effort."

The President contemplated the statement for only a moment before asking aloud, "Rationing?"

"Exactly," came Baruch's reply.

I separated my invisible self from the President for the remainder of the meeting, which went smoothly enough. Much of the discussion centered on working with various heads of industry to help them move toward military production. Although it would entail massive changes, rather than "crippling" any industry (this is the word Baruch had used), it was possible that corporate profits and payrolls might even see an increase.

Next on the agenda was a lunch meeting with Admiral Ernest J. King, who had recently been appointed commander of the United States fleet. I must confess that the frugality of meals served even within the Oval Office was somewhat embarrassing. Lunch consisted of cold soup, some semblance of chicken salad, and those damnable bread-and-butter sandwiches. To his credit, the admiral made no mention of the meager rations, but from his thoughts, it became clear he believed them to be a step below even the most limited of mess halls.

Later that afternoon, Roosevelt made a call to Secretary of State Cordell Hull to discuss the final draft of the Joint Declaration that was to be signed by the central Allied powers fighting the Axis alliance (Germany, Italy, and Japan). That was followed by a brief doctor's visit and then a return to the White House for cocktails and dinner.

During my initial visit, it had become immediately clear that these pre-dinner cocktails were a Roosevelt tradition. Most often, the President himself enjoyed mixing martinis and the like but for more formal occasions, his focus was on entertaining his guests. That evening he sat in his favorite rattan chair with Churchill on his right, and British Admiral Sir Dudley Pound on his left. Eleanor had seated herself on the far end of the parlor with Bishop Atwood, Reverend Peabody, and several others who referred to themselves as "annual fixtures" for this New Year's Eve tradition.

To be sure, the British admiral was an elderly and somewhat dour old man, but I had heard the Prime Minister tell Roosevelt in private, "He is the best brain in the Royal Navy." I stood before the three and simply listened to the conversation. Alonzo Fields, the ever-smiling head butler, was nearby, perfectly balancing a tray with one hand and serving cocktails with the other. He was dressed for the occasion in a black coat and tails and soon handed the President his drink.

"Your martini, Mr. President."

Franklin smiled joyfully, "Thank you, Fields!"

The Prime Minister was next, "Mr. Prime Minister, your Red Label Whiskey with sparkling water."

"Very good," came the reply. Churchill held the glass in his left hand, and the cigar in his right.

The admiral was served last, "Your bourbon, admiral."
"Most appreciated."

As Fields took his departure, Roosevelt took hold of
the conversation, "I know, I've never told the admiral
here . . ." he patted the admiral's armchair next to him
as he spoke, "but Winston did I ever tell you about
the time I asked Fields where I could find Eleanor?"

Lines appeared on the Prime Minister's forehead
as pondered the query and inhaled from his cigar, "I
do not believe so."

Roosevelt chuckled to himself and described the
occasion, "I was looking all over for Eleanor to ask
her one thing or another—I can't even recall what
it was—but in any event, I had looked through the
residence and couldn't find her. She wasn't in her
office. She wasn't in the kitchen or the Green room.
I couldn't find her anywhere! I had been calling out
'Eleanor!' and 'Babs!' Still nothing. I have to say, I was
a little frustrated by the time I finally ran into Fields
there on the first floor and still hadn't found her."

He turned back and forth between both men and
confessed, "Now, Eleanor will say that she had told
me where she was going, but I apparently wasn't
listening. She had gone up to Jessup, Maryland to
visit the Women's Correctional Facility up there.
Anyway, when I saw Fields, I asked him, 'Fields,
what happened to my wife?' His reply was matter of
fact, 'She's gone to prison, Mr. President.' I told him,
'Well, I'm not surprised, but what did they take her
in for?'"

He laughed heartily, and his smile broadened from
side to side, as both the admiral and the Prime Minister
laughed as well. Although I had heard the story
previously, I could not help myself from grinning, for
the President's laugh was most contagious.

While I stood there admiring the man before me, out of the corner of my eye, I suddenly caught a glimpse of a shadowy figure cautiously moving towards us. I turned and caught my breath as the ghostly form of Ruth #7 moved in my direction. Her vaporous extremities were swirling beyond her form as she crept ever closer to my side. When she finally stood beside me, it was evident that her eyes were exactly the same as Ruth #7, but the look upon this face appeared somewhat less troubled than the Ruth I had come to know.

"You must be Ben," she said.

I responded as a query, "Ruth?"

"I have wanted to speak with you."

I uttered the first thing that came to mind, "How did you find me?"

"Emmett speaks often of you and your whereabouts," came her reply.

I moved to inquire further, but she silenced me with a motion from her hand, "I don't have time. Emmett will be here any moment. Can you meet me on your approved timeline—the morning of January 1, 1942?"

I started to nod just as she said, "I have to go." In the next instant, she took a Horologium in her hand, whispered just under her breath, and vanished.

I had been standing there for no longer than perhaps two or three minutes when Emmett, the League's former Keeper of the Records, materialized in the room and began walking toward me. He appeared much the same as the last time I had seen him, with long white robes that fell to the floor, and thick strands of snowy hair that barely touched the top of his shoulders.

I waited to speak until he had reached me, "It seems you are making a habit of this."

At that moment, Fields announced that dinner was being served. Churchill and the admiral rose from their chairs, and Fields assisted Roosevelt in standing so that the President could give the appearance of walking as much as he was able—holding onto the cane he had been given with one hand and the butler's arm with the other. Eleanor and the others promptly departed for the dining room, as well.

When the room was empty, save for our own ghostly forms, Emmett's deep voice informed me outright, "This will probably be my last visit. I have come to ask you one last time whether or not you have decided to spend eternity with us?"

I shook my head in refusal, "You have yet to even discuss what it is you want from me."

Emmett appeared thoughtful before offering a reply, "Although your request sounds reasonable enough, too much information could undermine the very work I plan to accomplish."

To be sure, I had no intention of joining with him and the others, but I pried nonetheless, "How can you expect me to come with you when I don't even know what you want?"

Emmett nodded, causing his hair to brush against his shoulders, "Fair enough. Let me say only that I have been attempting to recruit a number of individuals on my own. Yet, in spite of my best efforts, there are some who have been reluctant to join me." He pointed his a robed arm in my direction, "I believe a diplomat would be most helpful in these discussions."

"I can't assist you in whatever you're doing."

"Why not?"

"It goes against everything that the Core stands for."

A surprised chuckle escaped with his reply, "I helped to create the Core!"

My head shook in refusal, "I will never join you."

"Very well, I cannot force you to become a part of this." He looked at me intensely and added, "But I promise you, I will get what I want one way or another. I will! If not from you, then by other means."

I asked him, "What do you mean?"

Emmett shook his head in refusal.

"Can you tell me how Emma #119 is doing?"

The query prompted another laugh, "I believe that Emma has become quite satisfied with her situation." He repeated himself, "This is the last time I will ask; do you wish to reconsider my offer?"

"I cannot."

"Then I must say farewell to you, my former friend, Ben #239."

A moment later, Emmett disappeared from my sight.

Shortly after my encounter with Emmett, I returned to the League facility for several hours of respite, as these time travel experiences take their toll. I chose to make no mention of seeing either Ruth's duplicate or Emmett. To be sure, these matters would be discussed when the time was right, and after I knew more. Although I was confident timeline XVIII was indeed a close replica to the ATL when I encountered Louise and Athena in the hallway (both headed toward the library for research), I told them that I had yet to make a decision about its suitability for Emmett's purposes. My thoughts for saying as much were twofold. In the first, these expeditions were essentially an exercise in futility, so my actual opinion made little difference. In the second, such a ruse became the perfect alibi for my meeting on the ATL with the other Ruth.

Following an all-too-brief rest, and thereafter undertaking the usual step-by-step time travel procedure, I found my vaporous self in the body of the President who was being quickly wheeled down the hallway on the second floor of the Executive Mansion by his secretary, Grace Tully. Her steps (and the wheelchair) came to an abrupt halt just outside the doorway to the Rose Room.

"You certainly seem to be in a hurry this morning, Mr. President," she said.

"Miss Tully, I need to talk with Winston as soon as possible! I have had the most wonderful idea. Go ahead and knock."

She reached out and tapped the door with her knuckles, "Mr. Churchill, are you up?" She waited a few moments, repeated herself, and knocked again. There was no response.

The President was impatient, "Just open the door. I'll push myself through."

Grace did as requested, allowing the President to enter the room alone. Once inside, she closed the door behind him.

Roosevelt looked toward the large, framed bed and its ruffled bed coverings, but no one was there, "Winston, where are you?"

There was no answer, prompting the President to wheel himself to the other side of the room, where he pushed open the bathroom door, "Winston, are you in here?"

My own eyes widened in complete surprise as the portly figure of the Prime Minister stood up in the tub, naked, dripping wet, and glistening before me.

Churchill was not upset in the least, "Good morning, Franklin," was all he said. He reached for a towel and began drying himself.

Franklin was slightly embarrassed, "I beg your pardon! I didn't mean to disturb your bath."

Churchill grinned, "The Prime Minister of Great Britain has absolutely nothing to hide from the President of the United States." He finished drying, and draped his robe about himself, inquiring, "What's on your mind?"

"I had the most wonderful idea, Winston," the President appeared joyful, "We should call the Allies, 'the United Nations.'"

The Prime Minister nodded in agreement, "Splendid idea, splendid."

Churchill walked through the bathroom door and reentered the Rose Room. Roosevelt followed close behind. Both men appeared animated as they began making plans to unveil this "United Nations" designation to the Allies as soon as possible.

I was already cognizant of the fact that the United Nations Declaration would be signed by the United States, the United Kingdom, the Soviet Union, and China later that very day. Prior to my departure on the first Roosevelt mission, personal research in the library had found that an additional twenty-two nations would all sign the declaration on January 2. In the midst of such thoughts, a female voice spoke my name from behind me.

"Hello, Ben."

I turned quickly and saw the duplicate Ruth standing within arm's length.

"Shall I call you Ruth?" came my inquiry.

She almost smiled with her response, "That may become confusing, considering you apparently know another. In Hebrew, the name means 'friend.' Perhaps you should call me Friend, or Ruthie."

My response was quick, "So you come as a friend?"

"I do. A friend from what is apparently called a lesser timeline."

I pondered aloud, "Did Emmett recruit you?"

Although her eyes sparkled with intensity, she frowned with her response, "In a moment of my own weakness, he did."

I motioned for her to proceed, "Tell me."

"I was an old woman, alone. Every member of my family had been gone for a very long time. For years, decades, I had been gathering records, and writing some of my own. My work was not yet complete. I lived in a cavern not far from the Salt Sea . . ."

I interrupted, "I believe it is now called the Dead Sea . . . I was there once."

She looked at me curiously.

I added, "For the Ruth I have come to know. I was there."

She nodded and continued, "I remember being awakened by Emmett. He promised that I could continue my work for as long as I desired." She held her timepiece in her palm before me, "I accepted the Horologium. Soon thereafter, I came to realize that I did not wish to be a part of what he was doing. Since he mentioned you so often, I decided that I needed to look for you. Will you take me back to this League of yours?"

I wanted to trust her. I needed to trust her. As I looked at her, I truly felt that I could trust her. I asked, "Can you tell me what Emmett is doing?"

Her reply was somber, "He plans to either rule the world or destroy it, and I am uncertain if, in the end, he cares which of these two he will bring to pass."

An individual's perception is not generally capable of the detachment and discernment required to ascertain the appropriate course of events for the ATL. Ultimately, that is the role of the CORE. It is far too difficult for any one person to set aside all thoughts, desires, and fears, and focus instead on what may be best for the Whole. For this reason, no Time Traveler is to make any decision regarding how best to change the past, or the most advantageous approach for creating the future.

Undoubtedly, as a Wayfarer you have already learned that many components of the third-dimensional world have an impact upon the perception of time. Two individuals attend a function (or take an identical journey) and the experience of each is quite different from the other. For one it appears prolonged, to another it is relatively brief. An enjoyable experience will appear to pass much more quickly than one that you dread. The malleable nature of time is not limited to perception. Scientific investigations themselves have repeatedly demonstrated the influence of motion, gravity, and even location upon the experience of time. All these things suggest that time is not an exacting standard; instead, it is a measurement, unlike anything you have encountered — a measurement interwoven with human consciousness upon the third-dimensional plane.

Excerpt, "The Malleable Nature of Time," *Wayfarer's Manual — Continuing Education (revised edition)*; **by Ruth #7**

EIGHT: *Journal Entry — January 25 ATL*

As it seemed the most straightforward approach to this new dilemma of what to call the duplicate Ruth, I quickly settled on the name "Ruthie." That said, my immediate priority appeared to be getting her inside the League facility and then taking her to see Ruth #7 without anyone realizing that she was, in fact, a duplicate. Getting inside the facility was simple enough, transversing the hallways without encountering someone who was with Ruth herself (or had just been in the company of Ruth) appeared to be my most challenging obstacle.

My sole advice to Ruthie had been simple enough, "Just nod and say hello, if anyone speaks to you."

"What if we encounter Ruth with others along the way?"

"Then we are caught from the start."

Any worry I possessed about being discovered proved to be pointless. My fellow graduates were nowhere to be seen — apparently elsewhere engaged in their respective time travel missions. We purposefully avoided any of the passageways that led to the Akasha library, where my own Athena was likely to be found. The sole individual we encountered along the way was Hakim #60, who smiled, briefly acknowledged our presence, and towered above us as he continued in the direction of the League Café.

When he had passed, Ruthie whispered, "Who was that?"

"He is Hakim. One of the kindest and most trustworthy members of the Core."

Ruthie appeared stunned, "He is the tallest man I have ever seen!"

I could not help but smile, "That was my initial assessment, as well."

When we arrived at the doorway to Ruth's chambers, I looked quickly around to make certain we were alone. (To be sure, it would become quite awkward if a passerby suddenly saw two Ruths peering at one another in the hallway.) When it was apparent that all was clear, I knocked on the door and waited. When there came no response, I knocked again.

"Ruth, are you in there?" I inquired. I was nigh unto opening the door myself to usher us both inside when I heard Ruth's voice from inside.

"I'm coming," she replied, opening the door only a moment later.

At first, the intensity of her eyes looked at me and then she gasped as she gazed upon the duplicate of herself.

"I want you to meet someone. Ruth, this is Ruthie."

She hurriedly ushered us both inside, "Come inside, quickly!"

She led us to the sitting area of her chambers, all the while having a very hard time removing her eyes from her other self. We took a seat, and it was Ruth who spoke first.

"I am sorry to keep staring," she apologized, "I had presumed this could be done but I never imagined that I would see it for myself."

Ruthie nodded, "It is somewhat unsettling. I find myself wondering how this is even possible."

Ruth #7 and I quickly glanced at each other, then Ruth explained, "Everyone here, as well as Emmett and the others, exist outside the boundaries of time. Emmett would have traveled to a lesser timeline to recruit you. From that point forward, your existence was no longer subject to the limitations of space or time." She paused for a moment and then added, "It would seem that you chose your appearance from the same period in life as I—when the children were young."

"I did," Ruthie concurred, and then a look of apprehension came to her, "Am I real?"

Ruth smiled, reached out her hand, and patted Ruthie's own, quickly comforting her, "Yes, I believe you are quite real."

I soon voiced what had been on my mind since first encountering the duplicate Ruth, "Now we can follow Ruthie to Emmett's alternate timeline!"

Ruthie was quick to disagree, "I don't know where it is."

"What?" I was perplexed.

"I don't know where it is," she repeated, shaking her head. "Emmett and Bruce called where we were a decoy . . . I believe they have several, and I think he is creating more than one alternate." Ruthie leaned forward and added, "Emmett has also been trying to recruit others."

"That is obvious," Ruth replied. "The question we must consider is who else and why?"

Ruthie leaned forward again and lowered her voice with the query, "Why do you think he chose me?"

Her reply was immediate, "As my replacement."

Ruthie pondered the response and then added, "I know he is planning to bring together some prominent people from history. He mentioned some names to Bruce, who seemed impressed, but most meant nothing to me."

"I think she is right," I acknowledged. "I saw him on my latest assignment. He said he wanted my assistance with diplomacy. He wanted help convincing others to join him."

Ruth turned to me in alarm, and then turned back to Ruthie, "Has he succeeded?"

She shook her head, "I don't know. But knowing Emmett, if he can't get someone he wants directly, he will try on other timelines. Emmett plans to recruit whoever he thinks he needs. He often told Bruce that they needed Ben, 'one way or another.'"

The thought disturbed me greatly.

After pondering the seriousness of the situation, Ruth asked me, "How did the two of you meet?"

I described our various encounters. First in the White House entryway, then near the kitchen, and finally in Churchill's bathroom when we had the opportunity to witness the Prime Minister getting out of the tub.

Ruth's eyes opened wide in surprise, prompting me to add, "It will forever be a memorable encounter."

Ruth then turned to Ruthie, "How did you find Ben?"

"Emmett spoke of him often and always seemed to know his whereabouts. I know he was getting information from someone here. At least that is what he told Bruce. I heard them discussing the plan to make Ben #239 a part of what they were doing, but he said that Ben kept refusing. That was the reason I decided to find him. I thought Ben might help me escape."

Ruth #7 inquired, "Who is Emmett getting his information from?"

"I don't know," Ruthie shook her head in frustration. "Although he had started to trust me, he had yet to take me fully into his confidence."

I asserted, "Emmett must have had some trust in you."

"Yes," Ruthie admitted, "but not entirely. I knew I needed him to trust me if I had any hope of finding a way out. He didn't tell me everything, but he trusted me enough to give me a Horologium. It has someone else's name on it, but it works."

The statement came as a complete surprise, "Whose name?"

Ruth reached out her palm and asked to see it for herself. Ruthie passed the timepiece, prompting Ruth to read the name aloud, "Francis #583."

I was confused, "Who is Francis?"

Ruth nodded, as though something had become quite clear, "That's how he did it."

"How he did what?" I asked.

Ruth looked to us both, "A Horologium is generated by the link between the ATL and the Akasha as soon as a candidate has been interviewed and approved for recruitment. Only that link can create the timepiece. Although Emmett is working on a duplicate of our facility, unless his timeline can take supremacy over our own, the only place he can obtain a Horologium is from here." She frowned, "This had to come out of the depository in the ATL Mission Office."

I was surprised, "Louise #217?"

"Or Milton #71," she replied somberly.

I repeated my initial query, "But who is Francis?"

Ruth passed the Horologium back to Ruthie as she spoke, "Do you remember when you arrived, and roommate assignments were being passed out?"

"Certainly, George and I became roommates."

She continued, "And do you remember why Emanuel got to have a room by himself?"

I recalled the occasion, "I believe we were told that Emanuel's roommate had decided not to take the Horologium. Therefore, Emanuel was by himself."

Ruth agreed, "Exactly. The roommate he was assigned had been Francis #583. He was an Italian friar. We believed that their similar interests in philosophy and things of a spiritual nature would make for an excellent match."

I reflected on what she had said for a moment until a thought came to mind, "Are you saying that whenever an individual decides not to become a recruit and take the Horologium, the watch is placed in storage? In the ATL Mission Office?"

"It is."

I was greatly disturbed, "Since the very beginning of the League, how often has this occurred? I mean, how many Horologiums might Emmett have at his disposal?"

She responded, "I have never considered the question." Suddenly, she appeared worried, "Perhaps a dozen . . . maybe more. I would have to think back a very long while."

Ruthie interrupted, "Why would Emmett take prisoners if he already has these timepieces? I thought he was taking prisoners for their time travel devices?"

"What?" both Ruth and I inquired at the same moment.

Ruthie repeated herself, "I thought Emmett had taken three prisoners so he could have their Horologiums."

Ruth was quite concerned, "Three? Who does he have besides Emma?"

Ruthie shook her head, "He never said their names. I never even heard the name Emma. All I know is that he and Bruce discussed three prisoners being kept on another timeline. I assumed one would be named Francis. Emmett never took me there. The only other person he ever mentioned was Sybil. I think she is watching the prisoners."

"There are three?" I pondered aloud.

"Yes," Ruthie agreed, "there are three."

Ruth #7 shook her head in dismay, "This is most disturbing."

Not long thereafter, I left the women in Ruth's chambers. It had quickly become apparent that the two wished to compare life experiences. There was much to discuss between them. When I departed, we all agreed that, for the time being, Ruthie would stay out of sight.

I walked most of the way back toward the café and was in the process of considering whether to make the journey to the Akasha library in search of Athena or return instead to my own chambers to look for George when I heard my name being called from behind.

"Ben, I need you!"

I turned to see George rushing down the hallway toward me.

"Why are you in such a hurry?" I asked when he reached my side.

Only slightly out of breath, he quickly replied, "I need your help."

"Absolutely, what do you need?"

He looked around as if to see if anyone else was listening, "I need help deciding what to wear."

As he stood completely attired before me, I stated the obvious, "But you are fully clothed already!" I reached out and pinched the front of his shirt between my fingers.

He smiled broadly and spoke that which came as a complete surprise, "I have a date for dinner . . . with Louise."

For a moment, I was truly dumbstruck. If Athena had asked me to name a dozen things that George might discuss with me before the day's end, a date with Louise would not have been on that list. I voiced the first thought that came to mind, "But you can't."

George suddenly appeared both perplexed and annoyed, "What? Aren't you the one that keeps encouraging me?"

As this was George, I admittedly had my guard down and nearly said too much, "That was before . . ."

"Before what?"

I couldn't say, "Before I discovered that someone in the ATL Mission Office was giving Horologiums to Emmett," so I replied instead, "You just returned from your latest mission. Aren't you exhausted?"

George peered upon my countenance with curiosity, "What are you up to?"

I shrugged, "Just feeling a bit tired myself. I would imagine that you might need a bit of stamina for an evening with Louise. Surely, you want to be prepared for such an encounter?"

"Sometimes you are quite annoying." George took me by the arm and began pulling me in the direction of our chambers. "I still need your help. It has been a very long while since I was on a date."

In the end, what George really desired was reassurance that the evening would go well. When we returned to our chambers, I suggested two or three different shirts that he might consider for his dinner with Louise. Each was met with some measure of rebuke, including, "I just wore that three days ago," and "I don't like the color." I quickly decided that even if Louise was involved in this business of Horologiums, there was little to be done about it just yet. I chose to encourage him.

"George, just have fun tonight."

He turned to me, looking somewhat nervous, "What if I don't know what to say?"

I patted him on the shoulder, "If you don't know what to say, ask Louise a question about her life. Asking someone about their life is a basic tool of diplomacy."

When he finally departed for his encounter with Louise, I made my way to the Akasha in search of Athena. I found her sitting at one of the tables, holding a tremendous volume that she was reading. Two other books lay on the table before her. As I approached her, I caught sight of the kindly-faced Gregory #143, who was exploring a shelf of books on his own. He waved, and I acknowledged him in return.

I turned to Athena, "What are you doing, my beloved?"

She looked up, and smiled, "Welcome back."

I bent to kiss her and then took the seat beside her. I repeated myself, "What are you doing?"

"Still trying to figure out how Emmett knew that Churchill would see a Time Traveler."

I jested, "You mean a ghost?"

She shook her head, "Whatever the Prime Minister thought he saw, I don't see how Emmett knew about it before the mission had even been assigned."

I reminded her, "Ruth told me that you had both come to the same conclusion. Emmett had to get his information from someone here."

Before she could respond, Gregory #143 came to the table and inquired, "I am running out of ways to feel useful. May I join you?"

"Absolutely," came my reply.

Gregory took a chair across from us. He pointed at the books before us, "What are you researching?"

"A most perplexing question," Athena replied.

I disagreed, "Ruth told me that Emmett got the information from someone within the facility."

Gregory looked confused, prompting Athena to explain, "Ben was at the Roosevelt White House. Winston Churchill was there at the same time. Churchill had been drinking quite a bit, and he was somehow able to see Ben as a ghostly presence."

Gregory's eyes opened wide in surprise.

"What we are trying to figure out is how Emmett knew this was going to occur even before the mission had been announced . . ."

I moved to speak but Athena stopped me with a wave of her hand, "Originally, Ruth and I surmised that

Emmett would have gotten the information from here immediately after it was assigned, but I remembered something that makes that conclusion impossible."

I was quick to ask, "What?"

"Do you remember when the commencement ceremony for graduation occurred?" she asked.

My response was certain, "On the ATL timeline, around the first part of December. I wrote it in my journal."

Gregory concurred, "That's right. That's when I returned to the League facility."

Athena nodded, "Ben, do you recall when your Eleanor Roosevelt assignment was chosen?"

"Absolutely. Milton said that it was chosen on the very morning of our commencement."

Athena nodded again, "In December."

"Exactly!"

She turned to look at Gregory and then back to me, "The problem is that you told me what Emmett said about the mission right after your first assignment with Sundiata Keita."

"I remember."

"The ATL is recording that mission as occurring in November. Emmett couldn't have gotten it from someone here. It hadn't even been assigned when he told you."

I was momentarily dumbfounded, but Gregory was quick to interject, "Then Emmett got it from the Akasha."

"He couldn't have," Athena admitted. "I have looked at every possibility."

Gregory turned to me and inquired, "Do you remember exactly what Emmett said to you about the mission?"

I thought back to my first appearance within Sundiata Keita's chambers and imagined Emmett standing before me. After a moment, I recalled aloud, "He said that he would check in on me again and then added, 'I was most intrigued by what happened on your Eleanor Roosevelt mission. It was the first time I have witnessed such an occurrence.'"

Gregory interjected, "He didn't mention that he saw you?"

I shook my head, "No, he just said that it was something he had not witnessed before."

Gregory added, "And this was a diplomatic mission?"

"Absolutely."

Gregory turned to Athena, "Regardless of when the mission was assigned, wouldn't the Akasha have indicated that there could be a problem that would need to be addressed?"

Athena twirled a few strands of hair between her fingertips as she listened and replied, "Yes."

"Then Emmett could have assumed that such a diplomatic mission would be assigned to Ben." Gregory pondered the problem a moment longer before speaking, "Isn't Emmett working with an alternate timeline — an almost duplicate of the ATL?"

We both replied, "Yes."

"Maybe Emmett wasn't talking about Churchill seeing a Time Traveler. Maybe he was talking about Churchill seeing a ghost. If his timeline is close to the ATL, then Churchill would have thought he saw a ghost on Emmett's timeline, as well. What if Emmett was talking about the Prime Minister thinking he had seen a ghost?"

Athena considered the possibility for only a moment, and then appeared overjoyed, "That has to be the answer! Thank you, Gregory!"

Although I was truly impressed with Gregory's reasoning, I was not as enthusiastic as my beloved, "That still won't help us find Emmett."

"It might," Athena replied excitedly, "but we're going to need help from the ATL Mission Office."

I had no idea what she was considering, "What are you thinking?"

"If we look at all of the 2,857 possible duplicate timelines that Grimwald originally discussed, can we discover how many of those timelines document Prime Minister Winston Churchill seeing a ghost? Emmett's alternate will be in that number."

I nodded and understood.

Later, when Athena and I were alone, I suggested we ask for help from the ATL Mission Office when we were certain whether it was Milton or Louise that could be trusted.

I was sitting in the classroom waiting for another of Agnes's required continuing education seminars to begin. With the exception of George, everyone was present. As I had spent the previous night (and much of the day that followed) alone with Athena, I had yet to see my sometime roomie. Agnes held her stylus in hand but had not written anything on the board. She paced back and forth, occasionally looking in my direction, as though I might be hidding some important information about my roomie's whereabouts. She had looked at me three or four times (each glance appearing more impatient than the last) when George finally walked in and took his seat.

Agnes was noticeably irritated, "Finally!"

George looked toward me, and I whispered, "How was the date?"

He smiled, "I think I'm becoming quite fond of Louise."

Agnes frowned, "Class has started." She took a deep breath, calmed herself, appeared to recollect her thoughts, and began to bob about with enthusiasm, "Tonight, I am going to tell you the most amazing story! Although it has long been considered a miracle, it is only a time slip." She slapped the top of her desk, "And this one occurred more than eighteen centuries ago!"

George quickly regained himself, "Is this a legend, or did it really happen?"

Our instructress pointed the stylus at him, "It is recorded by history in the Quran, by Christian scholars, by the Persians, in parts of Asia, in Turkey, in Greece, and in the Tartar language in parts of today's Russia." Her words were conclusive, "It is history!"

She turned to write five words on the board, underlining them twice with her stylus, "The Seven Sleepers of Ephesus." When she had finished, she turned back and added, "Now some people call these individuals 'The People of the Cave' but even though the name is different it is the same story. I need to give you some background information."

Just under his breath, George whispered, "No doubt."

Agnes continued, "The story begins with the Roman Emperor Decius. This occurred in the year 250 A.D., as measured on the ATL. At the time, there was a growing number of Christians who were practicing their new religion." She looked upon each of us in turn, "You must already know that the Roman gods had been around since the time of the Greeks, nearly 1,000 years before. This religion of Christianity was really quite small and certainly unimportant by comparison. Most Romans ignored the tiny Christian sect, but others were far less tolerant. For that reason, many Christians kept their faith a secret, but Emperor Decius soon passed an edict that made that impossible."

Agnes nodded her head in the affirmative but said no more. She simply looked upon us and waited. After a moment or two, I saw Manuela and Bonne Soeur Marie turn to each other, and finally, it was Bonne Soeur Marie who raised a hand into the air.

"Qu'est-ce que c'était . . . What was it? What was this edict?"

Our instructress was quite pleased, "Very good. I like an attentive class!" She resumed, "The edict declared that all citizens of the Roman empire would be required to make a sacrificial offering to both the emperor and the Roman gods in order to verify their allegiance. Now, this was problematic to the Christians because their religion prohibited such sacrifice. Decius also decreed that failure to make the offering would result in either torture or execution."

Agnes added her thoughts on the matter, "I guess it depended on the seriousness of the offense. In any event," she waved the stylus before her, "citizens were informed that everyone would be called upon to make this offering, and they would receive a certificate from the empire once the requirement had been completed."

Emanuel started to raise his hand but instead spoke aloud, "Madame Agnes, the edict could not have lasted for long. It would have wiped out all of Christendom!"

"Exactly right, Emanuel," she said proudly. "You are always thinking ahead! Decius only lived for a year or so after his edict—not nearly long enough to even give a majority of the empire time to take part in such foolishness. Obviously, the closer you were to Rome itself, the sooner you had a problem." She sighed, "Quite a number were tortured and killed. Even Pope Fabian himself was among them. The Catholic Church recognizes Pope Fabian as a martyr because of this."

George added his own thoughts, "Truly, I am most disturbed by what happened but what does any of this have to do with a time slip?"

Agnes frowned but reassured him, "I'm getting to that! Now where was I? Oh yes, I'm going to tell you about the seven sleepers." Our teacher turned to write seven names on the board. When she had finished, she spoke them aloud, "Maximilian, Martinian, Dionysius, John, Constantine, Iamblichus, and Anthonius. These are the seven sleepers of Ephesus. Sometimes, they are called the seven youths."

"Now Ephesus was one of the largest cities in the Roman empire," she continued. "It was a seaport. Emperor Decius decided to visit the port. Because the city's governor wanted to impress the emperor and prove that Ephesus was just as important as Rome itself, the governor posted the edict and declared that the sacrificial offerings were to begin immediately."

She paused for a few moments and began pacing before us. After walking back and forth several times, she pointed the stylus at the board, calling attention to the seven names, "I neglected to tell you that these young men were part of the Ephesus military . . . the Roman empire always had a military requirement for its male citizens. And these seven young men were very close to each other—they had grown up together. They were friends, and each of them was very devoted to the Christian faith." She waved the stylus, "It was a secret they kept to themselves."

She slapped her palm on the top of the desk with a bang, exclaiming, "But the secret got out! Someone within their unit—the Romans called it a century—turned them in, and they were called before the governor. They were commanded to offer a sacrifice to the emperor and the Roman gods, and each of the seven refused. For that offense, the governor sentenced them to death."

She continued, "They were ordered to be taken to the Ephesus prison to await their execution . . ." Agnes turned toward Emanuel, "The Romans called these public prisons Custodia Publica." She turned back to the class, "Thankfully, for the young men, the soldiers who escorted them were members of their own unit, and they were friends. They thought the governor's sentence much too harsh, so they allowed the seven to escape, telling their superiors that the seven had gotten away with help."

"The seven escaped the city and headed towards the mountains. It was there that they found a cave and decided to hide inside. This is where the story really gets interesting!" Our instructress bobbed with enthusiasm, "While this was happening, two other things occurred at the same time. One . . ." she tapped the stylus against a finger, "unbeknownst to the seven, one legionary—that's what they called members of a unit—had seen the seven young men escape and secretly followed them out of town. He knew where they were hiding."

Agnes tapped a second finger with the stylus, "Two, the ship carrying Emperor Decius came into port. During Decius's visit, the governor learned that these seven Christians were hiding inside the cave, so the governor asked the emperor if he would like to witness the execution. Decius offered an alternative.

"'Seal the cave with stone and opus caementicium. Let them die from hunger and thirst,' the emperor said." Agnes looked at Emanuel, "Opus caementicium is what they called cement." Turning back to the class, she waved the stylus repeatedly, "That is exactly what happened! The cave was sealed shut, and a plaque was posted outside inscribed with the names of the seven young men. It detailed their crime and their suffering as a warning to others!"

My roomie appeared upset, "How does that story have anything to do with a time slip?"

Agnes slapped her desk, "I'm not finished yet!" She shook her head in frustration, "After the cave had been sealed, the young men fell asleep . . . oxygen was still getting in there somehow but there wasn't a great deal of it. They fell asleep but they didn't die, and while they were sleeping, they went through a time slip. In an instant, the seven traveled from 250 AD to 445 AD — one hundred and ninety-five years later!"

Manuela interrupted, "But they were still sealed inside the cave!"

Agnes smiled, "In 262 AD Ephesus had a tremendous earthquake that leveled most of the town. That earthquake jarred loose both the stones and the cement, so when the young men woke up, they were able to get out of that cave. They journeyed into town and were obviously shocked by what they saw — the city was entirely different from the one they had left behind. Decius was long dead. The new emperor was named Theodosis. Perhaps the biggest surprise came when they found was that Christianity had become the state religion!"

"Eventually, their story got out." She explained, "These young men started talking about their miraculous experience. They showed the people the Roman coins they had from the time of Decius. They took countless individuals to the cave. Local bishops came to hear the story. Word spread throughout the continent that such a miracle had occurred. Now these people had no knowledge of time travel or time slips. They had to explain the experience with things that were familiar to them. Instead of time travel, they believed that the seven had been put to sleep and then resurrected nearly 200 years later by Jesus Christ himself!"

Agnes ended the tale by shaking the stylus at each of us in turn, "This story spread far and wide as proof of the resurrection. That is the Seven Sleepers Time Slip!"

I found myself quite surprised by the outcome, "It suggests that one could remain in an alternate time after a time slip."

"Exactly!" She appeared pleased.

George was unconvinced, "Couldn't this all be nothing more than a legend?"

"Is it?" Agnes was undeterred, "Many legends are based on fact. Why don't you ask Athena to look into it?" She nodded in the affirmative, "Athena knows everything."

Bonne Soeur Marie raised her hand, but our teacher brushed it aside, "It's time for class to end." She suddenly frowned, "By the way, Nashwa informed me that she has not heard from any of you about possible suggestions for new recruits. These need to be turned into her office immediately!"

George whispered, "I thought that was voluntary?"

Agnes relaxed herself and then added, "I have decided to give you a special treat for one of our upcoming seminars!" She looked around the room for some evidence of enthusiasm, finding none she continued, "I am going to let each of you give a brief report on your next assignment . . . That should be fun!"

George's reply was predictable, "You have got to be kidding!"

*In the physical world, there are those who have come
to believe that science — above all else — is the greatest
approach to any knowledge one might possess. It is an
ongoing source of information and data. It provides a means
for observation, experimentation, and the exploration of
evidence and theories that can lead to that which may be
true. It has transformed medicine, history, and even life
itself. Certainly, it is responsible for tremendous leaps in
human understanding, traceable as far back as the ancient
world. However, science has done very little to understand
the nature of time, for science chose to separate itself from
the exploration of consciousness, and consciousness is the
very thing to which time is ultimately bound.*

*Consciousness cannot be weighed. It cannot be observed
by physical sight. It may not be the same tomorrow as
it was today. It is generally imperceptible to the very
tools science relies upon to measure and observe. To the
scientific mind, consciousness is at best an enigma; at
worst, it is irrelevant. Because of these presumptions,
science has never understood that all that exists is an
expression of consciousness. Until science embraces this
one fundamental truth, the nature of space and time will
remain unknown, for time itself arose from consciousness.*

**Excerpt, "Various Scientific 'Theories' Regarding
the Feasibility of Time Travel," *Wayfarer's Manual —
Continuing Education (revised edition)*; by Ruth #7**

NINE: *Journal Entry — February 2 ATL*

As a week had already passed since Agnes
informed us that no one had come forward with recruit
recommendations, upon rising (and even before having
my muffin and coffee) I decided to visit Nashwa's

office as my first priority. To be sure, immediately upon hearing Nashwa's initial request, I contemplated a number of possibilities — possibilities from my time travel missions, possibilities from my life, and even possibilities from history. I must admit that individuals from history with whom I had no personal familiarity gave me the least measure of confidence. How could I choose someone with whom I had never had a personal interaction of any kind? It also seemed preposterous to suggest a king, a prince, a pharaoh, or any individual who had become accustomed to unlimited power and decisiveness. How could such a person function in the League, deal with supervision, or attend Agnes's never-ending classes? I considered over a dozen candidates who seemed to possess potential, but in the end, one name continually rose above all others, and it was that individual I recommended without reservation.

I let myself into Nashwa's office and found her sitting behind her desk.

"Good morning, Ben #239," she replied cheerfully.

"Good morning," I responded, "I have come with a recommendation for your list of possible recruits."

She seemed pleased and smiled, "Who is it?"

I nodded, "She is committed. She is trustworthy. She is kind-hearted. I would trust her unconditionally. . ."

Nashwa interrupted, "That's quite a recommendation coming from you. Who is it?"

"Her name is Noor Inayat Khan. Some call her Nora Baker. She was a member of the French underground during the Second World War."

"I have heard the name," Nashwa assured me, and then smiled a second time, "Thank you for the suggestion. I will start working on it immediately."

"Thank you."

I smiled back, and then headed in the direction of

the League café, as both a coffee and a muffin awaited me.

I arrived at the café just as my fellow Wayfarers were assembling. Athena and Louise had just come to the table with their food. I took a seat at one head of the table, with Athena on my left. George took the seat on my right, with Louise sitting next to him. Such an arrangement was becoming quite common for our group. Although I occasionally pondered Louise's possible involvement in this matter of taking Horologiums from the ATL Mission Office, she and my roomie were becoming inseparable. I found myself hoping that she was not somehow involved.

I looked at my muffin, honey, and coffee, and then turned to see Athena's ever-present breakfast fare — yogurt and fruit. George was most fond of toast, eggs, and sausages, and Louise generally took a small biscuit with an apple or figs. My remaining classmates gathered around the table in turn. After everyone had taken a bite or a sip of that which lay before them and exchanged morning pleasantries, Soeur Marie spoke excitedly.

"Bonnes Nouvelles . . . good news! I saw Agnes in the hallway this morning, and she told me we are going to receive our latest assignments tonight!"

George frowned, "Oh joy. I have been hoping for another mission."

Bonne Soeur Marie remained enthusiastic, "Not one of those all-hands-on-deck assignments — a real mission!"

"Great," came his reply, before taking a bite of toast.

A thought came to mind, which I spoke aloud, "Louise, do you ever help Milton pull these mission assignments together?"

Louise sighed, and shook her head, "I used to when I first got the job, but not now. Milton likes to decide everything dealing with time travel himself. I don't know what's going on most of the time. My job is not as fun as it used to be."

Athena turned her head in surprise, "What?"

"I said the job is not as fun as it used to be," Louise repeated. "I'm thinking about finding something else to do."

Athena waved her hand from side to side and exclaimed, "No, I'm wondering why Milton isn't telling you anything. That doesn't sound like Milton, at all."

I turned to Athena and concurred, "Didn't you use to tell me that you really liked working for Milton, because he kept you informed about everything?"

"Absolutely," my sweetheart agreed.

Louise shook her head in frustration, adding, "Well, he's not like that anymore. I think this whole problem with Emmett has changed him." She shrugged, turned back to George, smiled, and began stroking the back of his hand.

My sweetheart and I looked at each other, and Athena spoke softly, "I will ask for her help on what we discussed with Gregory."

Following our group breakfast (and after both George and I had embraced our companions and allowed them to depart for their respective duties), the two of us walked side-by-side in the direction of our chambers.

I turned to him, "Can I ask you something?"

George was quick to reply, "Louise and are getting along quite well . . ." he looked at me, "but that is all I am saying."

I smiled, "No, not about Louise. I want to ask you about the Core."

He was perplexed, "I imagine Athena would be a much better source of information on that topic."

I assured him, "I am looking for your opinion, not a detailed discussion of the Core's activities. If I asked you to name the members of the Core who were most important to the League and this work, who comes to mind, and why?"

"That's easy. First on my list would be Ruth #7. Not only is she the author of our texts, but she understands this work better than anyone. I would also include Milton #71, because he has long been the mission supervisor and League historian. I would then add the Governor-General, Sara #11." He turned to me with a query, "Why do you ask?"

My reply was straightforward, "I wanted to see if your answer would be similar to mine."

"And was it?"

I nodded, "George, not only were the names the same, but my listing was in the very same order."

I was hurrying in the direction of Ruth's chambers when suddenly I saw one of the two Ruths walking alone in the hallway in front of me. (I must confess that I was completely uncertain which one.) When I narrowed the distance between us, I reached out my hand and grasped her shoulder.

"Ruth? Ruth #7?" I inquired.

A faint smile formed on her face, "Yes, Ben, it's me."

I looked around to make certain we were alone, "Where is she?"

"Where she's supposed to be. In my chambers."

I nodded in approval, and we journeyed the remaining short distance in silence. Once we arrived at her doorway, Ruth opened it, allowing us to venture inside. The duplicate Ruth was nowhere to be seen, prompting Ruth #7 to speak aloud.

"Ruthie, I'm back. Ben's here with me."

Ruthie entered through a door that led to another room, "Hello, Ben."

I looked between them, still fascinated by the situation of two identical Ruths, and replied, "Hello, Ruthie." I was quick to motion toward the sitting area, "I have something extremely important to discuss with both of you."

After we had each taken a seat, I spoke the very thoughts that had filled my mind for much of the morning.

"I wish to share a number of matters that I have been contemplating."

Ruthie was the first to respond, "We're listening."

I began, "Less than an hour ago, I asked my roommate, George, to name the most important members of the Core. He said, in order, Ruth #7, Milton #71, and Sara #11."

Ruth interrupted, "That was most kind of him."

"While pondering the same question, I had come up with the identical three names, in the exact same order. I imagine that Emmett would list these very names himself."

I leaned forward to emphasize my subsequent point, "It occurs to me that if Emmett could take over the Core, he would no longer face any opposition to achieving whatever it is he hopes to accomplish. To be sure, the Core and the League are all that stand in his way. Let us call this matter number one."

I resumed, "Perhaps the most straightforward approach to controlling the Core might be to eliminate — or better yet — replace those very individuals who are in key administrative roles." I pointed toward Ruthie, "In spite of the fact that Emmett's plan was not a complete success, we already know that he obtained Ruth's duplicate. Let me suggest that he is either in the process of doing the same with Milton and Sara or he has already done so. Let us call this matter number two."

I turned first to Ruthie, "I don't know if you are aware, but I have been in a relationship with our current Keeper of the Records, Athena, for quite some time."

She simply listened.

"Athena is extremely intelligent. In fact, Agnes, our instructor, is quite fond of using the expression, 'Athena knows everything.' When Athena and I first got together, she told me that Milton #71, the ATL Mission Supervisor, told her everything. If the truth be told, he may have said a few things to her that should have, perhaps, remained a matter of Core business."

Ruth #7 looked at me inquisitively, so I added, "Such as how your Horologium was being tracked by the Core."

She shrugged, as though the offense was of little consequence.

"Since Athena left her position working with Milton," I continued, "the job has been undertaken by a French woman named Louise #217." I added my personal critique, "You might describe Louise as being extremely outgoing. In any event, during breakfast, Louise complained that Milton had changed a great deal since she first took the position. She said that Milton doesn't tell her anything anymore, especially when it comes to issues regarding time travel. I shall call this matter number three."

Ruth #7's eyes opened wide with surprise, "I find that hard to believe. It doesn't sound like Milton at all." "No, it does not," I concurred. "Nonetheless, it is one of the matters before us. In terms of matter number four, ever since it happened, I have repeatedly found myself amazed, even astounded, that Emmett would take Emma #119 to be a part of his efforts." I turned to Ruthie to provide her with additional background information, "Emma was a member of the Core, who got herself demoted for spying on other Core members. Even on the best of days, she is extremely disagreeable."

I turned to Ruth, looking for confirmation or disagreement, but she said nothing, so I continued, "There is absolutely no reason I can fathom why Emmett would want to have her on his alternate timeline. It is illogical," I leaned forward for emphasis, "and from what I have seen for myself and heard from others, Emmett considers himself a man of logic." I repeated, "As I said, this is the fourth matter that has been on my mind."

The two Ruths continued to watch me closely as I revealed the next matter.

"When Ruthie arrived and displayed her Horologium, inscribed with the name Francis #583, it became apparent that someone within the ATL Mission Office had taken it from storage and given it to Emmett. The only individuals who had access to these Horologiums are Louise and Milton. One of these two is somehow involved with Emmett. This would be matter number five."

I next turned toward Ruth #7, "Do you remember how we first learned that Emma #119 was missing?"

Ruth nodded, "It was after your graduation commencement. We were having the celebratory meal when we heard the news."

"Exactly," I concurred. "I had been looking around for Milton and couldn't find him anywhere. As I recall, he had been gone for quite some time. It was only after the meal was well underway that he suddenly ran into the hallway to proclaim to us all that Emma had been taken."

Ruth #7 moved forward and inquired, "What are you suggesting?"

I stated the only conclusion that had been on my mind for the preceding hour, "In terms of matter number six, let me suggest the following for you to consider. What if Emmett came to League headquarters on the day of commencement when he knew all of us would be engaged? What if he came to replace Milton with a duplicate as part of his plan to take control of the Core?"

Ruth #7's reply was most reasonable, "How could he be certain that he would find Milton alone?"

"I cogitated upon that very issue several times over, and then it suddenly came to me. Milton was not alone. Emma was somewhere nearby—that's the only reason she was taken. She got in the way of their plans for an abduction. They had no choice but to take her."

I spoke with certainty, "When Milton ran into the banquet hall and announced that Emma was gone, he was not our Milton. Instead, he was the very duplicate that Emmett had recruited to replace him. I would wager that one of the three prisoners being held by Emmett, Bruce, and Sybil is our own Mission Supervisor, Milton #71."

Both Ruths appeared quite shocked by my litany of matters, but it was Ruth #7 who said, "Ben, this is all quite disturbing."

"I agree, however, I do believe we have one piece of good news, which I will call matter number seven."

Both women looked toward me as if grasping for a thread of hope.

"While Athena and I were in the company of Gregory #143, he postulated the most interesting possibility regarding what Emmett meant when he told me, 'I was most intrigued by what happened on your Eleanor Roosevelt mission.'"

Ruth #7 was becoming fascinated.

"He suggested that Emmett wasn't talking about Churchill seeing a Time Traveler at all; he was talking about Churchill seeing a ghost — something that he had no doubt witnessed on his own timeline . . ."

Ruth #7 was quick to interrupt, "We need to discover the number of timelines where Churchill thought he saw a ghost! Emmett will be on one of them."

I nodded approvingly, "That is exactly what Athena said, and she has gone to ask Louise to research that very issue." As the time seemed right, I added a personal request, "Obviously, I have spoken with Athena about this seventh matter, but because of our vow to keep Ruthie's presence a secret between us, I have not discussed any of the other six. I would like your permission to do so."

Ruth was quick to agree, "I think that would be wise." She seemed to ponder a thought for only a moment before adding, "I believe the time has come to tell our Governor-General, as well."

In spite of everything else that was on my mind (including the fact that I had yet to get Athena alone to discuss the six matters I had shared with both Ruths), I have to admit that I found the topic of our required continuing education seminar that evening quite interesting. Agnes provided us with a narrative of perhaps seven or eight of the most popular, yet fictitious accounts, of time travel, time slips, and supposed time travelers, all dating from around the twentieth century (as measured by the ATL). The point of her discussion was simply that each of these tales had turned out to be completely false. To my complete astonishment, however, even after their falsehood had been publicly declared, countless individuals continued to spread these fictitious stories on such things as the "internet," the "web," and all manner of "social platforms." (George has been only moderately successful in explaining each of these as "a kind of Akasha device.") I found myself intrigued by both the narratives and this ongoing act of distribution because they suggested an extremely intense desire on the part of numerous individuals that this business of time travel would turn out to be real. (I can personally attest to the fact that it is.) My roomie voiced a very different assessment, "Why are we having this discussion? These are nothing more than fabrications, fantasies, and lies!" In any event, I have chosen to record two of the most memorable stories herein.

After finishing each of the tales in her presentation, Agnes made a tremendous showing of wiping the board clean of all that had gone before and beginning anew. On one such rendition, after cleaning the board before us, she grasped the stylus and quickly wrote out "Antelope Springs Time Traveler," underlining each of the words twice over.

"I am going to tell you the story of the Antelope Springs Time Traveler," she assured us.

As this was the fourth tale, she had narrated thus far that very evening, my roomie was quick to provide his thoughts on the matter, "This is no more real than the others. Right?"

Agnes peered at him intensely, "Just let me tell it!" And then, turned back to the board to write the word "Fossil" and continued.

"I assume that most of you know what a fossil is, but just in case, it is the remains of a long-dead plant or animal that has been preserved in sand, mud, and water." She waved the stylus before us, "Whatever has died becomes like stone, or leaves an impression of itself in the hardened rock. Some call it petrified. That's a fossil."

Her narration resumed, "According to the ATL, in the summer of 1968, a fossil hunter by the name of William Meister found what appeared to be an enormous, fossilized rock. When he tapped it with his hammer, the top portion of the rock split off. He was totally amazed by what he saw underneath!" She leaned forward and spoke as though revealing a tremendous secret, "He had exposed the imprints of two human feet. These footprints even appeared to have been wearing sandals or shoes, and the fossil was obviously millions of years old! William was very much surprised, and probably wondered, 'Did humans wear coverings on their feet back then?'"

She bobbed about before the class while informing us, "Perhaps he planned to ask other fossil hunters if they had ever seen something similar. When William looked more closely at the footprints, he was shocked! He couldn't believe what he saw right there in front of him!"

Soeur Marie was quick to inquire, "Qu'est-ce que c'était? What was it?"

Agnes's reply was a matter of fact, "It was a trilobite. A trilobite that looked like it had been walked on and crushed by one of those two feet."

"A what?" Manuela was the one who spoke.

"A trilobite," Agnes repeated.

George spoke up, providing us with additional background information, "They're small crustacean-looking creatures . . . no bigger than the end of your thumb." He held up his thumb and continued, "The first trilobite fossils were found just before the year 1700, off the coast of Wales. They've been extinct for hundreds of millions of years."

Agnes appeared quite surprised, "That was excellent, George! Very well done!"

(I wish to note that George was unable to hold back a grin.)

Our instructress continued, "Now from what George has just told us, why was William Meister in a state of shock?"

Emanuel's hand rose high into the air as he responded, "The answer is obvious. How could a human being have stepped on a creature that had been extinct for hundreds of millions of years? There were no such thing as a human when trilobites were alive."

Agnes brought the palm of her hand down hard on the top of her desk with a bang, "Exactly! So, what does that imply?"

There was silence until I suggested the only logical answer that came to mind, "Maybe this individual was a Time Traveler? Perhaps this Time Traveler had journeyed back to some long-ago beachfront that was now part of Antelope Springs. While walking along, that Time Traveler stepped on that trilobite and indented both footprints and that little creature there in the sand."

Agnes nodded and bobbed with excitement, "That's the answer exactly . . . At least, that's the answer that spread throughout much of the American continent and beyond. The news traveled like wildfire. The story got quite a bit of notoriety and was repeated by thousands. People who had never even thought about the possibility of traveling through time began to ask, "Is time travel possible?"

Agnes shook her head, "Imagine, even when the whole thing was discredited, the story was passed around for years."

I was quick to inquire, "How was it discredited?"

Agnes pointed her stylus at me, "The fossil was examined by several paleontologists — these are scientists who study the earth and its fossils. They all reached the same conclusion. Yes, there was a crushed trilobite there in the petrified stone, but there were no footprints. Those scientists identified the two imprints as natural rock formations, not feet. Rocks, not toes, had killed that little trilobite."

Agnes slapped the top of her desk to emphasize the end of the tale, "That is the story of the Antelope Springs Time Traveler!"

Perhaps thinking that his time could be better spent in the company of Louise, George shook his head in dismay, "I'm not sure why this is important to our required ongoing continuing education."

Our instructress pointed the stylus at him and appeared ready to speak but instead simply shook her head in frustration, turned, and began to wipe the board clean.

The second tale I choose to recount was discussed at the very end of our class. On the perfectly clean, whiteboard before us, Agnes wrote and underlined, "The Hakan Nordkvist Time Slip." She then lifted a single piece of paper from her desk.

"I want to read the story just as Hakan Nordkvist told it in the year 2006, as measured on the ATL. These are his words." She nodded twice, and began, "'It all happened on the afternoon of the 30th of August. It was a beautiful day, and I was on my way home from a job in Färjestaden.'" Our instructress looked up briefly, "That's a small town in Sweden. 'When I got home, I found water on the kitchen floor. There was a leak. I got my tools and opened the doors to the sink and started to work. When I reached in to examine the pipes, they seemed to be further in than I remembered. I had to crawl inside that cabinet, and as I did so, I discovered that it just continued, like a tunnel. I kept on crawling further and further inside. At the end of the tunnel, I saw a light, and when I got there, I realized I was in the future.'"

Agnes looked up to make certain we were still listening, and then resumed her reading, "'I met myself as a 72-year-old. The year was 2042. I tested myself to see if it was really me. And the strange thing is that he knew everything about me. Where I hid my secret stuff when I was in first grade, and what the final score of the school's soccer match was in the summer of '88. He knew it all. We even had the same tattoo, although the one he had was a little faded. He told me some of the stuff that will happen in the future, but not much. I even made a film with my cell phone of the two of us together . . . I don't care if people think I am a liar. I know I'm not. I met myself in the future, and if this happened to me, surely it could happen to someone else . . .'"

My roomie was the first to query, "Are there really pictures of them together?"

Our teacher was most certain, "There are. In fact, a digital movie of two balding men — one old and one quite young, each having the same tattoo, was passed around countless times."

Emanuel pondered aloud, "That might be a most fascinating experiment."

"What kind of experiment?" Manuela was intrigued.

Our studious Swede responded, "To take pictures on one of our mission assignments and bring them back here."

I was intrigued, "That does sound most interesting. It would be one way to bring evidence from one timeline to another."

Bonne Soeur Marie came next, "Bonne idée! Good idea! I think we should do it!"

George added, "I would be open to giving it a try."

Before anyone could say more, there was a loud bang as Agnes slapped her palm on the top of her desk, "We're getting off track!" She waved her stylus about, "The point is that this story is false! It was a marketing campaign by an insurance company, suggesting that individuals needed to make plans for their futures. Imagine!" She was disgusted, "Using the subject of time travel for such foolishness! Anyway, even after the origins of this story came out, it was spread by countless individuals for many, many years!"

Bonne Soeur Marie started to raise her hand in the air, but Agnes waved it aside, "It's been a long night, and it's time to stop." She reached inside her dress pocket and began to unfold a piece of paper as she informed us, "I have your newest mission assignments." She read aloud.

"Ben #239, destination Sofia, Bulgaria, 2295, in the matter of Viktoria Petrova and her diplomatic initiatives with North America."

"Bonne Soeur Marie #304, destination San Giovanni Rotondo, Italy, 1921, in the matter of Padre Pio and his hospital."

"Emanuel #41, destination Shiraz, Iran, 1844, in the matter of the establishment of the Bahá'í Faith."

"George #111, destination Braga, Portugal, 2117, in the matter of the philanthropic efforts of Camila Costa."

"Manuela #64, destination Cappadocia, Turkey, 374, in the matter of Gregory of Nyssa and his sermons on human equality."

She bobbed one final time as she proclaimed, "Class dismissed!"

Throughout your involvement in the League, the questions that will arise may be many. Over time, those questions will change, evolve, and sometimes resurface themselves. Reflecting back upon my own long experience, I can share that on frequent occasions each of these thoughts has entered my mind: Who am I? What is the purpose of life itself? What is the nature of personal consciousness? Is the consciousness of which I am aware my own, or is it part of something larger than myself? Is everything I think I perceive nothing more than a perceptual illusion? WHO is the Author of Creation?

I must admit that the answers to these very questions have changed with the passage of time. They have grown and expanded and eventually simplified themselves until my perception of the answers became such that I have often pondered aloud, "Why didn't I always know this to be true? I finally understand! This is all so simple!" With the hope that this will be of assistance to others, here is what I have come to know. The universe consists of One Being, One Consciousness, and One Moment in Time, and each of us is part of that Whole.

Excerpt, "Time Travel and the Components of Consciousness," *Wayfarer's Manual—Continuing Education (revised edition);* **by Ruth #7**

TEN: *Journal Entry—February 11 ATL*

I should make note of the fact that it was only two or three days after my last journal entry that Athena and I found ourselves sitting at her table, relaxing alone within her chambers. Suddenly, the sound of a knock came upon her door, and I rose to open it. Immediately, I was greeted by a waft of French perfume and an anxious-looking Louise standing before us. She pushed herself through the entryway, hurried past me, and rushed toward the table to speak to Athena.

Quickly, I closed the door and followed close behind.

"I must beg your pardon for taking so long with this question." Louise sighed, "I could only do the research when Milton was elsewhere engaged."

Athena assured her, "We completely understand."

As I had been awaiting this very moment for several days, without exchanging even a single pleasantry I found myself asking, "Did you find anything? Did Prime Minister Churchill really see a ghost on multiple timelines?"

Louise shrugged her shoulders, "I cannot say whether or not Churchill really saw a ghost. What I can tell you is that he thought he saw a ghost, and it happened on more than one timeline."

Athena leaned forward, "Tell us what you found."

"I started with the 2,857 timelines discussed by Professor Grimwald—those that had never received a time travel mission. You asked if it was possible to discover on how many of those Churchill believed he had seen a ghost." Louise nodded, "It took some time to calculate all of the possibilities, but between our office resources, the Akasha, and a little investigation on my own, I finally found the answer."

I was impatient, "How many?"

She responded, "There are 137 timelines on which Prime Minister Winston Churchill reported to his wife or someone else that he had seen a ghost in the Roosevelt White House."

We finally had an answer, and Athena appeared quite pleased. She rose from her seat and embraced

Louise, "Thank you, Louise!" She turned to me and stated most assuredly, "Emmett's alternate timeline will be one of those. We need to tell Ruth #7 and Sara #11 immediately."

The next two days became a whirlwind of activity. Obviously, our first priority was informing Ruth and the Governor-General that Grimwald's listing of possible locations for Emmett had been reduced tremendously. During that brief encounter, Sara requested that Athena and I refrain from discussing the presence of the duplicate Milton with any member of the Core or any other Wayfarer. Her rationale was obvious.

"We cannot let Milton know that we know about his connection to Emmett. It is important that we find this alternate timeline as soon as possible!"

Ruth's counsel was for each of us to maintain our regular routines, "We must act as if everything is normal, and as though absolutely nothing has changed."

Sara interjected, "That's very good advice. We don't want to alarm the incoming students."

Her pronouncement came as a complete surprise, "New students? The recruits are here already?"

"Not yet, but they'll be arriving very soon," the Governor-General responded.

Athena stopped twirling the strands of hair between her fingertips and turned to Ruth #7, "Do we know how many there will be?"

Ruth nodded, "Nashwa is finalizing all of the arrangements as we speak. It appears we will have four new recruits this semester."

"Who are they?" I quickly inquired.

The Governor-General brushed aside my query, "You'll both meet them soon enough. In the meantime, there is a great deal we need to accomplish."

To be sure, our normal routines included the newly assigned time travel missions. Obviously, that entailed personal research in the Akasha library. Shortly thereafter, not only did I find myself exploring the subjects of Victoria Petrova and her Bulgarian homeland, but I had to set aside time for some semblance of understanding regarding the world in the 23rd century. For her own part, Athena became completely engaged with assisting five Wayfarers in researching their newest mission assignments. It goes without saying that during such times of preparation and planning, meals were eaten only when we were able, occasions of camaraderie and conversation were all too rare (if occurring at all), and anything dealing with the shaking of the sheets became absolutely nonexistent.

The days that followed included a great deal of personal effort on the part of each Wayfarer. That effort included multiple trips to the library, assistance from Athena, a thorough examination of the problem, and ongoing cogitations upon possible solutions. Once this personal research had been accomplished and sufficient background information obtained to ensure the best opportunity for a successful outcome, we were ready.

Emanuel was the first to depart, followed by Manuela, and then Bonne Soeur Marie. When the others were gone, George and I stood within the library bidding farewell to one another. (Earlier that day, he had given a goodbye embrace to Louise, and I had done the same with Athena.) I turned to my roomie, wishing him well.

"Bon voyage, George. Good luck in Portugal."

He nodded, "Thank you, Ben. Remind me where you are going?"

"A place called Sofia, Bulgaria."

Shortly thereafter, I took my Horologium in hand, began the travel process, and disappeared from the library only a few moments after George.

Rather than providing a complete narrative of my experience with Viktoria Petrova in 2295 Bulgaria, it's probably sufficient to impart the summary I gave to Agnes and my fellow Wayfarers on the very night of our continuing education seminar, occurring right after we had all returned. I will then describe what followed.

Our instructress began by choosing to depict the evening's agenda in the same manner she had done nearly a fortnight before.

"Tonight, we're having a special treat!" She bobbed about enthusiastically. "You all get to describe your latest mission assignments!" She added quickly, "Since everyone will be speaking, please keep your comments to no more than fifteen to twenty minutes per person. Who wants to go first?"

I could not help but be surprised when George raised his hand. Agnes appeared even more astonished.

"George?" She looked at him curiously and then seemed to recover. "Well, yes. Absolutely. If you want to go first, you may do so!"

George shook his head no, "I have a question."

Immediately, she seemed fully back to herself, "What is it?" she demanded.

"Is this session being recorded?"

"George, you know as well as I that everything that happens anywhere is recorded by the Akasha! Why are you asking?"

He continued, "You told us these continuing education sessions were required. Maybe some of the Wayfarers who have been doing this kind of work much longer than the rest of us are bored with these kinds of personal presentations . . ."

She interrupted, "Tonight's seminar is optional for them!" She shook the stylus at him and continued before he could say another word, "For anyone who is not in this room, it is optional. Now, who wants to go first?"

It was no surprise to see Emanuel stand and head toward the front of the classroom. Agnes passed him the stylus and took a seat for herself. He quickly wrote three words on the board: "Báb," "Bahá'u'lláh," "Bahá'í," and then turned to face us.

"My mission was to help ensure the beginning of the Bahá'í faith," he said.

Bonne Soeur Marie looked around the room to see if anyone appeared to have knowledge of the name he had just spoken, and then raised her hand. He pointed in her direction.

"Soeur Marie, I will clarify everything in a moment." He then provided us with an explanation that quickly enabled us (and any who might be watching later) to understand the faith, its beliefs, and his assignment.

According to our Swede scholar, the Bahá'í faith began in Persia. (As background information, Emanuel explained that in 1935, Persia changed its name to Iran.) In 1844, a young Persian man said that he had suddenly become aware of the fact that he was to be the forerunner of a new faith that would bring peace, enlightenment, and a universal understanding of God. He then changed his name to "the Bab," which is Arabic for "gate."

The beliefs he espoused focused on the unity of God, the unity of religion, and the unity of all humankind. Such teachings were met with widespread enthusiasm, and it was not long before he was followed by ever-growing numbers of people. In spite of his charisma, he promised the crowds that an even greater Messenger than himself would come—one who would embody the fulfillment of the world's religions. Obviously, that kind of message was viewed as heresy in 19th-century Persia, and more than 20,000 followers of the faith were eventually executed for their beliefs, including the Bab himself. In spite of this harsh and ongoing persecution, various disciples continued to spread the messages of the Bahá'í faith.

Emanuel described how his mission assignment focused on helping the Bab and his various disciples escape, remain alive, or stay hidden for as long as deemed necessary by the ATL. One of those disciples was Mírzá Husayn 'Alí, who had left a life of wealthy privilege to become one of the Bab's messengers. In 1952, he was arrested, beaten, and imprisoned in Tehran. After four months of capture, he was released and banished from the country. He fled to Turkey, where he lived for the next ten years. It was there that he realized he was the very Messenger that the Bab had foretold. He next journeyed to the Holy Land, where he would live out the remainder of his life for the next 30 years, writing the holy texts of the Bahá'ís. From that day forth, this religion of faith, inclusion, and peace continued to spread. Emanuel's mission assignment had been accomplished.

He concluded with a simple statement, "Since that time, this religion of unity and peace has maintained its headquarters in Haifa, Israel, and has grown to millions of followers."

As was customary for these group presentations, we four Wayfarers applauded enthusiastically. Afterward, Agnes remained seated, saying approvingly, "Well done, Emanuel. Next?"

Before anyone could raise a hand or rise from their seat, I quickly stood and walked to take the stylus from Emanuel's hand. I dutifully wrote the word "Bulgaria" on the board, underlining it twice, and then wrote "Technology," "Agriculture," and "Pharmaceuticals." Underlining each in the same manner. I turned to see Agnes nodding in approval from her seat.

Although I began by confessing how I had felt somewhat out of place in a century that seemed most comfortable with virtual interaction, holographic projection, and AI automation, I quickly explained my overall task, "My mission was essentially twofold. First, to ensure that Viktoria Petrova became trade ambassador, because the ATL maintains this as a most crucial step in ensuring her role as Bulgaria's president ten years later. Secondly, these trade negotiations between North America and Bulgaria were quite sensitive in terms of international relations."

I then pointed the stylus at each of my classmates in turn, just as our instructress might have done. (I should note that she smiled and nodded approvingly.) "You see, Bulgaria had longstanding ties with both the New European Union and NATO." I quickly turned, wrote, and then underlined both sets of initials on the board: "NEU" and "NATO." "It also maintained a centuries-old connection with its sister city in Ontario, Niagara Falls. Preserving a relationship with both Europe and North America, each with its own goals and opinions, is not always an easy matter."

For the subsequent quarter of an hour, I occasionally bobbed about in front of my fellow classmate, enthusiastically explaining the various trade negotiations and outreach that Viktoria Petrova had initiated and expanded. Those projects included a massive increase in solar panel exports, ongoing pharmaceutical manufacturing and distribution, and, of course, a massive increase in the global sales of wheat. I then made special note of the fact that after experiencing a steady decline in population, the country of Bulgaria had stabilized at around 5 million citizens, reminding my listeners, "That is about twice the size of the American Colonies in 1776."

I finalized my presentation by announcing, "I am pleased to report that my mission assignment was a complete success!"

After standing in place to wait until all applause had come to an end, I placed the stylus on top of Agnes's desk and returned to my seat.

George watched me closely, shook his head, and spoke loudly enough so that only I could hear, "You are such a suck-up!"

Agnes stood and announced proudly, "Oh, Ben, that was exceedingly well done! Thank you for a most enjoyable presentation!"

I smiled.

At that very moment, the alarm system went off.

The deafening sound of the buzzer reverberated throughout the entire facility, making any attempt at communication completely futile. Agnes walked to the front of the room, and then looked toward the classroom door and waited. The intensity of the noise continued. After several minutes of glancing at the doorway, she began to appear impatient. The ringing continued, with our teacher having little to do but grip the end of her stylus and wait. She looked to the doorway again, hoping for news from the ATL Mission Office. Until that was received, there was no way of knowing what type of emergency confronted us. The incessant alarm seemed to go on and on. Finally, Milton #71 appeared in the doorway.

Noticeably out of breath, his English accent was barely loud enough for us to hear, "Let me apologize for the delay . . . here is your emergency assignment!" He passed the pages to Agnes, and turned to leave, still out of breath.

Agnes took the pages between her hands and started to read them to herself. Just as quickly as it had started, the alarm suddenly came to an end. She sighed and started reading aloud from the beginning.

"Ben #239, there are problems on timelines VI, XLII, and LXXV. We need a diplomat! Elizabeth I has failed to sign a death warrant executing Mary Queen of Scots, and Mary's supporters are now planning to place a Catholic Queen upon the British throne!"

As soon as the words had been spoken, she looked toward me and then back at the pages held between her hands, "Didn't we already have this emergency during our first semester?"

The same thought entered my mind as I moved toward the front of the classroom. She looked back at her pages and continued.

"There is more . . . Emanuel #41, a dozen timelines are showing major disruptions in Anglican Church history. This will rejuvenate a revival of Catholicism throughout the British empire." She shook her head in frustration, "This is in complete opposition to the ATL and has to be stopped immediately!"

Emanuel had just started moving toward the front of the room to join me when Agnes looked at the pages again and yelled, "Wait! Bonne Soeur Marie #304, we may need a healer to assist the wounded and dying. War is looming between England and Spain!"

Agnes waved the pages before us, "We've seen this before! This is a big one! We have to move quickly!" She frowned angrily, and shook her head in disgust,

"This has got to be Emmett! Someone needs to eradicate him!"

I watched George tell Manuela, "I think it's time to help the colony on Roanoke Island again," just as Agnes motioned for Bonne Soeur Marie, Emanuel, and me to come closer. She began walking nervously around us, saying the same words she had said so many times before.

"You have prepared for assignments like this. You know what you are doing! You do know what you are doing?"

Shortly thereafter, we three journeyed on our separate missions into England's past.

Upon my arrival at Whitehall Palace, it became readily apparent that Emmett (or one of his other deserters) had already influenced Her Majesty, the Queen. I stood within the figure of Elizabeth I as her thin fingers brushed themselves against the skin of her face, long disfigured from the scars of smallpox and the lead-laced makeup that would eventually contribute to her death. William Davison, her royal secretary, stood nearby, pointing to the execution warrant and quill that he had placed on the table before them. Davison pleaded, yet again, for her to sign the document.

"I fear you have no choice in this, Your Majesty." His words were somber, "There is no question of Mary's part in the conspiracy."

I focused for a moment to separate myself from the Queen, just as she insisted, "No! I will not be responsible for this. Mary is my cousin." She pushed the document to the other side of the table.

Davison watched her closely and pondered his words before replying, "Although a cousin, she chose to involve herself in this plot against you. You must set aside these feelings from the past. She can no longer be trusted. We have no other course of action."

A myriad of thoughts raced through the Queen's mind. Not only was Mary a cousin, but the two had once called each other friend. Although Mary had been forced to abdicate the Scottish crown in favor of her son, executing a former queen would undoubtedly lead to even more problems — problems with the Pope, problems with Catholics in Spain, problems with some of her own people. Surely, there was recompense for regicide. At the very least, she would face the wrath of history, if not divine will. She had already been the focus of three assassination attempts, and the Pope had excommunicated her, calling the legitimacy of her reign into question. Above all else, Elizabeth desired to be remembered for her accomplishments, not these issues of conflict and duplicity, and certainly not the death of a rival.

Davison continued to reason with his Queen. He calmly presented one argument after another. There was no wiser course of action. Elizabeth's ongoing reign was in the best interest of the empire. Spain would use Mary as a pawn; its sole desire was to place a Catholic on the throne. Parliament itself had declared Mary guilty of treason. He discussed a litany of arguments and then began to repeat himself.

It was while he was speaking that I used my own Wayfarer's influence to persuade Her Majesty that she had little choice in the matter. I closed my eyes and focused, pulling from Elizabeth's own mind the very words I hoped to convey. I let the feeling of those thoughts come to the forefront of her consciousness. I dwelt on the words repeatedly, compelling her to do the same.

Finally, Elizabeth sighed, "I fear there is little choice in the matter." She reached out and took the document in one hand, dipped the quill in the ink with the other, and affixed her signature to the warrant.

Her words were somber, "Neither choice is without consequence. If another way can be found to set this threat aside, I pray it be given every consideration."

Davison nodded in agreement as he took the document in hand. He then turned to leave her chamber. It seemed that my mission was complete.

To my great surprise, however, all at once things began to change before me, and I stood witness to something my time-traveling eyes had never seen before. Time itself appeared to rewind, and everything I had just observed suddenly began to move backward. Davison retraced the steps he had just taken and nodded in reverse as he placed the document back into the hands of the Queen. Next, Elizabeth appeared to speak somberly, but the words were gibberish to the ear, as they, too, were spoken in reverse.

The Queen placed the writ of execution on the table and seemed to be signing her signature in reverse, from the right to the left. The quill's ink was removed from the page itself as she wrote. William Davison spoke his own gibberish, as his cautionary arguments were verbalized in reverse. When he had finished, I felt the prattle of the Queen's thoughts race through my mind — thoughts of regicide, and the Pope, her own legitimacy, and the imminent death of a cousin whom she had once called friend. I watched Davison rewind more of his own words until I suddenly became aware of a figure dressed all in white, standing in the chamber before me. The ghostly form of Emmett had appeared.

I was astonished, "What did you just do?"

Emmett shook his head, prompting his long, white hair to dance upon his shoulders. He was not pleased, "Do you really think that you, or any member of the League, can stop me?"

"What did you do?" I asked more vehemently.

Emmett pointed a finger at me as he spoke, "Although you and the others may be free from time, they are not." He turned to point at Elizabeth and Davison, both still speaking and both completely oblivious to the ghostly presences standing nearby. His words were firm, "I used my influence and undid everything that had gone before. You just watched time rewind and reverse itself. In the end, know that all of your efforts will be futile."

I demanded, "I have heard that you're holding three prisoners. Who are they?"

My words startled him. He opened his eyes in surprise and sounded even angrier as he spoke, "I do not have time for this! You and the others have already caused far too many problems. I am warning both you and the League."

"What about the prisoners?"

He frowned, "Leave me be!" In an instant, he was gone.

I stood quietly for only a moment, contemplating the fact that for the first time ever I had seen Emmett truly unsettled. As my mission still lay before me, I turned back to watch Elizabeth and Davison repeat the very scene I had witnessed upon my arrival.

He pointed to the execution warrant, pleading his counsel, "I fear you have no choice in this, Your Majesty. There is no question of Mary's part in the conspiracy."

The Queen spoke with certainty, "No! I will not be responsible for this. Mary is my cousin." She pushed the document aside.

The secretary watched her closely, practicing his words in his head before he spoke, "Although a cousin, she chose to involve herself in this plot against you. You must set aside these feelings from the past. She can no longer be trusted. We have no other course of action."

As before, many thoughts raced through Elizabeth's mind. She and Mary were cousins and had once called each other friend. The problems she already faced with both Spain and the Pope were bound to get worse. What would history think of an act of regicide? Would Mary's execution prompt another attempt on her own life, or even death itself? Above all else, she desired to leave behind more for the empire than she had received when she herself had become Queen. She could not help but feel such was her destiny.

Davison's words were both calming and supportive. He explained the reasons why this was their only course of action. It was best for the empire. It was best for their relationship with Spain. It was best for her people. As he began to repeat himself, I focused my Wayfarer's influence upon the same argument Davison had used from the first: there was no other choice to make. I closed my eyes, concentrated, and pulled from the Queen's own thoughts the very opinion she had repeatedly held in mind.

All at once, Elizabeth sighed, "I fear there is little choice in the matter." She took the document in one hand and the quill in another. A moment later she had affixed her signature to the warrant.

When all was once again in accordance with the ATL, I returned to the League.

I materialized in the Akasha library, just as my shoulder was grabbed by Athena. I could see that she was unsettled.

"I've been waiting and looking for you everywhere!" She exclaimed, taking me by the arm. "Sara wants to meet with us as soon as possible." She pulled me toward the double doors exiting the library.

Still recovering from the journey, I asked only, "What's going on?"

"I don't know," was all she would say.

We hurried through the various corridors and hallways leading to the administrative offices. I wanted to tell her about my most recent encounter with Emmett but rationalized to myself that I would need to repeat the very same tale once we were with the Governor-General. We journeyed through one passageway after another, with Athena asking me once if I was okay after the journey, and then speaking softly to herself, "I wonder what Sara wants?"

The rest of the journey was filled only with the sound of our footsteps. We passed the League Café and then journeyed down the long hallway of administrative offices. First came "Personnel," followed by "Recruitment," "Student Services," "Recordkeeping," and then "Meeting Room 1," where we rushed inside.

Sara sat on one side of the table with Ruth #7 sitting beside her. The Governor-General pointed to a couple of chairs across from her and asked us to take a seat.

She said only, "We have a problem."

I repeated my earlier question, "What's going on?"

This time it was Ruth who spoke, "We're waiting for someone else to join us."

I nearly inquired, "Who is it?" But the look of concern on their faces suggested that it was perhaps more expedient to wait until I knew what had prompted the meeting. Silence filled the air until, finally, a knock came upon the door.

Sara spoke up, "Come in."

The door opened to reveal Nashwa standing before us. She looked around the table at the four of us sitting in silence, and then turned to Ruth and Sara.

"Sorry for the interruption but you wanted to know when the new students were here. They've arrived and are in their first class with Agnes.

"Very good," came the Governor-General's reply.

Nashwa turned to leave and began closing the door. Suddenly, she stepped aside to reveal ATL Mission Supervisor, Milton #71, standing in the doorway. He entered the room, closed the door behind him, and took the seat next to Ruth.

He said, "Sorry for the delay, my friends, but it has been quite a day to be sure."

Sara nodded and then pointed at Athena and me, "Milton can you share with Athena and Ben what you came to tell us earlier today?"

"Certainly," he replied. Rather than his usual disposition, his words were filled with concern, "I told them that Louise was behaving quite differently of late. She has not been herself since the student commencement."

I glanced at Athena and then leaned forward to inquire, "What do you mean?"

Milton reflected aloud, "It was little things at first. She used to ask all kinds of questions, and we discussed everything. Suddenly, she didn't talk as much. She seemed more focused on personal matters." He paused and then admitted, "There were several times when I came to the office for one thing or another and found her there. When I asked her why she was working so late, she would only say, 'Research.' Looking back, I should have reported it sooner."

.

Ruth interjected, "Did you look into the issue of the Horologiums?"

He appeared despondent, "I'm afraid you were right. I had eleven locked away. The Horologiums are gone."

The Governor-General was quick to inquire, "What about Louise?"

Milton sighed, "I have looked everywhere. She is no where to be found."

Ruth turned to me. Her words shook me to the core.

"Ben, you were correct in all things but one. It wasn't Milton that Emmett replaced on the day of our commencement . . . It was Louise."

Sara added, "We can be certain that she already alerted Emmett that we know about Churchill and the 137 timelines. In fact, it seems clear that the Elizabethan emergency was simply his way of keeping us all occupied while they set a new plan in motion."

Athena was greatly disturbed by the news, "What can we do?"

It was Ruth who spoke. Although her eyes sparkled, she was obviously distressed, "We have to get Louise back . . . the real Louise. We'll be calling a meeting shortly to discuss plans."

The reality hit me, "I have to tell George!"

The Governor-General agreed and then turned to Ruth and inquired, "Do you think Emmett will change timelines, or should we keep looking on the 137?"

"Creating an alternate timeline is not an easy matter," Ruth spoke assuredly. "We need to keep looking. He may change timelines, but it will take him a very long time to create one that is suitable." She added, "We also need to tell the rest of the Core about what has transpired, including the presence of Ruthie. She has decided to stay."

Sara replied simply, "Very good."

After I had detailed the most recent encounter that I had had with Emmett, and answered a few questions, Athena and I departed from the meeting room and quickly turned down the hallway leading to my chambers. We had to find George. As I had recovered my strength from the travel mission, our pace was swifter than our arrival.

"We need to tell him together." Athena's words were filled with concern.

I nodded, taking her hand as I led us quickly around the next corridor. All at once, I ran us both into a woman coming from the opposite direction. She gasped, straightened her horned-rimmed spectacles, and looked me straight in the eye.

"Young man, there is something very wrong with you!"

I was completely shocked, "Emma?"

"Remind me of your name?"

I managed, "Ben #239," before inquiring, "How did you get here?"

Athena quickly added, "Are you okay?"

"No, I am not okay! I was held against my will."

I repeated, "How did you get here?"

Emma angrily shook her head, "It's not your concern, but Bruce let me go!"

"Did you see Louise?" Athena managed to ask, as Emma pushed past us both.

"Louise who?"

She walked away in disgust, speaking angrily, "I need to see the Governor-General."

As she left in the direction of the administrative offices, Athena and I continued our hurried pace. Before we had even reached the League Café, however, we saw George running toward us. When he reached us, he came to an abrupt halt, waving an envelope before us.

"She's gone!" He said, "She left me a letter."

Athena spoke first, "I am so sorry, George."

"I'm sorry, my friend. We didn't know she was a duplicate."

George looked at his envelope and then turned back to us, "She said she loves me."

"I am so sorry, George," Athena repeated.

"We have to find her!" My roomie exclaimed.

I shook my head, "George, she works for Emmett. You can't be with her."

George was flabbergasted, "I'm not talking about her . . . the duplicate."

I was confused, "What? I don't understand."

His words were quite earnest, "If the duplicate Louise loves me, it stands to reason that the real Louise loves me too! We have to find Louise #217!"

Athena reassured him, "That is exactly what Ruth and the Governor-General are planning. We're leaving as soon as we can."

"We're with you on this, George," I comforted him. "We're coming with you."

Within the hour, I found myself standing outside the doorway to Agnes's classroom. I could not help but smile when I heard the very words that she had spoken on my first day of class.

"Imagine the difficulty each child faces trying to overcome the illusion of time when from the very first that child is presented with the perceived notion that everything follows a particular schedule!"

Agnes's words were filled with enthusiasm, "There is a time for birth; there is a time for death. There is a time to get up; there is a time to go to bed. There is a time for work; there is a time for play. The dates on a calendar are thought to contain some measure of meaning. There is a time to celebrate birthdays and holidays, beginnings and endings. All of humankind is caught up in a nonsensical measurement directing the course of their lives! And it is an illusion each of you will learn to conquer."

While she was finishing, I stood outside the doorway and waited. It was only a few moments before four students (wide-eyed and seemingly overwhelmed) left the classroom and walked out into the hallway. Several pairs of eyes looked at me, and I greeted them, but it was the young Indian woman I chose to approach.

I inquired, "Can I ask, who was your personal recruiter?"

She looked at me, appearing somewhat startled, and replied, "Hakim. He is the tallest man I have ever met!"

I nodded, "He's been described that way before."

She reached out her hand to take my own, "I am Noor Inayat Khan. You can call me Nora."

I grasped her hand for a moment and replied, "It is very nice to meet you, Nora."

She looked at me and smiled, "Although you appear younger than the drawings I have seen, your portrait is well-known throughout the city of Paris. You are Mr. Franklin, aren't you?"

I smiled in return, "Here they call me Ben #239. You can call me Ben."

A Note to Readers:

Many aspects of the historical incidents detailed within Alternate Timeline are true, including philanthropy's role in addressing the coronavirus in the Philippines and Noor Inayat Khan's involvement in the French resistance. Winston Churchill did make a secret visit to the White House during the 1941 Christmas season and New Year, and there are, in fact, multiple accounts of the presence of Lincoln's ghost during the Roosevelt administration and later. The Carl Jung Time Slip was experienced by Jung, but he believed the experience was a connection between two unconscious minds. Edward Hale's 19th-century booklet, *Hands Off*, is considered one of the first tales to describe an alternate history created as a result of time travel.

For those who are interested, many of the theories regarding the nature of time proposed by Relativity, wormholes, and Closed Timelike Curves can be Googled for additional information, as can the Nechtansmere Time Slip and the story of the Seven Sleepers of Ephesus.